A PRACTICAL MISTRESS

Mary Brendan

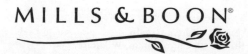

MILLS & BOON®

First published in Great Britain 2006
Harlequin Mills & Boon Limited,
Eton House, 18-24 Paradise Road, Richmond, Surrey TW9 1SR

© Mary Brendan 2006

ISBN 0 263 19036 6

Set in Times Roman 13 on 16½ pt.
08-0306-61133

Printed and bound in Great Britain
by Antony Rowe Ltd, Chippenham, Wiltshire

A PRACTICAL
MISTRESS

Chapter One

'How dare you even think to treat your sisters so abominably!'

'Now, steady on, Helen, I don't like your tone. You know I am not legally obliged to house you and Charlotte, or give either of you a penny piece.'

'Not legally obliged, perhaps! Morally obliged indeed you are, and not simply to house us, but to keep us in comfort, and you cannot pretend you don't know it.'

George Kingston seemed unaffected by the mixture of disgust and entreaty firing his sister's tawny eyes. In fact, he lounged back in his chair and continued to probe his teeth with a little silver toothpick.

Helen Marlowe, née Kingston, felt her stomach churn with impotent rage as she observed her brother's apathy. Tendrils of raven hair were angrily twitched back from a complexion that, customarily pale as porcelain, was flushed with righteous indignation. 'I know you do not truly want to be mean to us, George, for I am certain you recall as well as

I the undertaking you gave Papa. We are not asking for *your* money, all we want is the allowance to which we are entitled. And I need not remind you that Papa stipulated Westlea House was to be a home for Charlotte and me for as long as we needed its shelter.' She paused to drag in breath to deliver a final conscience-pricking truth. 'Our parents would be distraught to know you are planning to sell the roof from over your sisters' heads.'

Helen's small fingers curled into her palms as she realised that her brother was more irritated than swayed by her appealing to his principles. Abruptly she swished about in a rustle of lavender dimity and addressed her sister-in-law. 'Have you nothing to say on the matter, Iris? Are you comfortable, knowing your husband seeks to eject us from our home?'

Iris briskly stepped to a gilt mirror to inspect her reflection. She tipped her hat this way and that on flaxen hair whilst making her snappish response. 'Another house will be found for you both. George has already looked at one. I can't understand why you and Charlotte would want to carry on so. You are comely enough to find a husband to support you, you know, Helen.' It was said with a slight frown, as though already she doubted the value of her compliment. Dissatisfied with the floral embellishment on her new bonnet she tweaked it some more. 'And Charlotte is quite a beauty. I'll wager the girl could net herself a man with good prospects. Perhaps a banker or the like might take to her.'

'Charlotte has a suitor. She and Philip are in love and want to announce their betrothal, as you well know.'

'How sweet. But he has no money, and no prospects, as you well know,' Iris countered acidly.

George Kingston plunged upright on noticing his sibling's darkening expression. He was well aware that, dainty-built as she was, Helen could act the virago when protecting her own or Charlotte's interests. As his wife and his sister locked combatant stares, he took the precaution of stepping across the rug between the two of them. He stuffed his hands into his pockets and rocked back and forth on his feet. 'It's not as though you and Charlotte will be homeless, Helen,' he coaxed. 'I've found somewhere for you actually. Just this afternoon I arranged a short lease on a property on Rowan Walk. Six months should be time enough for you both to make your own arrangements for the future.'

'Rowan Walk?' The tone of Helen's voice was initially aghast. A moment later she repeated the address in a voice that had lowered threateningly.

'Yes,' George spluttered, conscious of the reason for his sister's simmering fury.

Rowan Walk was not situated in an area where genteel women would choose to reside. In fact, he was aware that it housed a host of females kept in modest style by wealthy gentlemen of the *ton*. Such fellows might like a mistress conveniently close to home, but they baulked at paying exorbitant Mayfair rates. The eastern suburb in which Rowan Walk lay was within easy reach. A lengthy carriage ride would thus not take up time destined to be more pleasurably expended. The neat terraces of townhouses in the vicinity were of adequate size and quality and, because of their association with demi-mondaines, very good value, too.

'If you think for one moment that Charlotte and I will move into such an area, you must be addled in the wits,' Helen announced. A glance at her sister-in-law revealed her to be maliciously amused. 'But perhaps you have not wasted your money, George. There might be someone you know who would appreciate an available house there.'

George tightened his lips—he understood the allusion to the latest gossip doing the rounds. He stabbed a low-lidded accusatory glance at his wife. Iris had the grace to flush and flounce about to primp some more at her appearance.

Iris had never used discretion in her quest for powerful and wealthy lovers. Helen often wondered if her sister-in-law relished the attention she got from being the butt of gossip. The fact that George quite obviously resented, yet regularly endured, being made to look a fool by his wife, was also intriguing to those, such as his sisters, who cared enough about him to ponder on it.

'Good grief, Helen, you're a widow, twenty-six years old, and it's high time you found another fellow to look after you and ceased being a burden on me!' George blasted out the reprimand, more in embarrassment than in anger. He had hoped his sisters might still be ignorant of the likelihood of him again being a cuckold.

A sour taste dried his mouth as he dwelled on his wife's current prey. Iris might deny it, but he knew she was infatuated with a man he detested. The same man who had been his enemy for many years.

His sisters rarely socialised; if news of Iris's latest infatu-ation had reached Helen's ears, then gossip was rife. Abruptly he stalked back to his chair to slouch into it. 'You may live on Rowan Walk or in the poorhouse, it makes no difference to me.' He raised a moody glance to his sister's tense features. 'And it serves you right for choosing to marry a pauper when you might have married well.'

'I thought we might come to that. It was exceedingly bad of me, was it not, to marry a man I loved when I might have married a man old enough to be my grandfather.'

'Scoville was dead within two years of proposing to you. It would scarce have been hardship to be a sick man's wife— a very rich sick man's wife—for such a short time. Had you given the decrepit old fool the heir he wanted, your future at nineteen years old would have been fine indeed.'

'I beg to differ. And I have no regrets that I married Harry. He was a gentleman who did not need money to recommend him. And I am not ashamed to demand again and again that you release to us what our father wanted us to have. If you resent me coming constantly to badger you for money, you have only yourself to blame.' Helen glowered at her brother from beneath eyebrows as lush and black as sable. 'If we are a burden on you, it is you who has made it so by withholding what is rightfully ours.'

George flushed beneath his sulk and snapped his head away from a pair of flaring golden eyes. Imperiously he said, 'If you continue to recommend that our sister encourage Philip Goode, Charlotte will go the same way as did you. Sentiment is all very well, but it doesn't pay the bills. The man has nothing to offer her.'

'He has the most important things to offer her: his love and devotion. Apart from which he is pleasant, polite and totally charming.'

'What a shame such a paragon cannot afford a wife,' Iris murmured with a cattish smile. The bonnet with which she had been fiddling was tossed aside in irritation. Bluntly she informed her husband and sister-in-law that she was going out shopping.

George stared morosely at the closed door before sighing with such unconscious sadness that a little of Helen's anger evaporated. It was ironic that George could, in all seriousness, criticise her for having wed unwisely when his own marriage was a mockery. At least she had been happy for the short time she and Harry had been man and wife.

Helen studied her brother in profile. He was a handsome man, his hair a similar shade of auburn to their sister Charlotte's. Although in his mid-thirties, George's complexion was unlined, yet his youthful demeanour was spoiled by a constant miserable droop to his mouth.

And little wonder he was miserable, for he had married a woman who seemed to relish making him look ridiculous. Yet Helen felt more exasperated than sympathetic. Despite Iris's callous infidelities, George seemed to be in his wife's thrall, for the baggage had no trouble twisting him about her finger.

But her brother was correct in one respect, Helen realised wryly. Sentimental memories were indeed an indulgence when one was struggling to persuade the butcher to extend credit so one might dine on offal. Harry had been kind and charming, but he had died leaving her with little more than her wedding ring and his outstanding army pay.

'Marlowe's been dead for seven years.' George shattered Helen's wistfulness with that harsh truth. 'You've had plentiful time for mourning. Now it is time to be sensible.' The toothpick was again between his teeth. Suddenly he pointed it at her. 'Iris is right: you are passably pretty. Dark looks were the rage last season, you know. I recall when you were eighteen and made your come-out, you received more than one offer that year.'

'My, what a fine memory you have, George!' Helen drily exclaimed. 'That was eight years ago and most of my suitors now have found wives. Besides, if you honour Papa's wishes and the trust he had in you, there will be no need for me to chase a proposal. I am not going to release you from your duty to us. Release our money and have done with it.'

George flushed and flung the silver tool down on a table. 'I have some unforeseen expenses at present and…and, besides, I am not legally obliged…'

'Ah, we have done that bit, George.' She sighed before saying reasonably, 'I would understand your parsimony if I thought you were honestly in trouble, but I know your wife fritters the money we need for essentials on new Paris fashions.' Helen's eyes slid meaningfully to the abandoned bonnet.

George lurched out of his chair. 'That's enough!' he roared.

He strode two paces back and forth. 'You know nothing of my life or my finances and I will not have you speak so of Iris.'

'What would you have me say, then, George?' Helen asked quietly. 'That it is not her new clothes you cannot afford, but her fondness for the gaming tables? Or perhaps her new landau has taken Charlotte's dowry?'

George swung about to stare grimly at his sister. His face now held the expression of a man resentful of unpalatable truths. 'I think you ought go before I say or do something I should not.'

Helen recognised her brother's torment and walked, head high to the door. 'You can dismiss me now if you want. But if our cash is not forthcoming in the next few days, I shall be back. We have no more credit at the merchants and have little stocks left of food or fuel. It is early spring and still quite cold.'

'If you are both determined to be leeches on me, then you and Charlotte can make a few blasted economies!'

Helen managed a smile tinged with bitterness. She glanced down at her waif-like body whilst recalling how plump had looked her sister-in-law's figure. Iris's arms and bosom had fair threatened to burst from the fine silk of her stylish gown. In fact, Helen thought acidly, if the woman did not curb her appetite she would be on the way to becoming fat.

'Charlotte and I have long since cut marchpane from our diets…' Helen noticed George's lips angrily writhe at the reference to his wife's liking for sweetmeats. 'And mutton has become a once-a-week luxury,' she truthfully added. 'What economies would you have us make, George? Already we make do and mend. Shall we boil up potato broth for every meal and live in the cold and dark?'

'A smaller property would cost less to heat and light. If you want to dine well, then it is sensible to move somewhere else.' George's reasoning was accompanied by an impatient whirl of a hand. 'The two of you seem more concerned with pretending you can afford to live in a fine neighbourhood than attending to your comfort.'

'That's not true!' Helen cried, outraged. 'Westlea House is our home. You know it holds dear memories of our parents. How can you be so cruel as to imply we care to keep up appearances?'

George seemed about to speak, but abruptly closed his jaw and showed Helen his back. He was not hiding his face, ashamed of his outburst. Nor was he uncomfortable knowing how frugally they lived, Helen realised. He was simply trying to shield his expression whilst summoning up another excuse for why she and Charlotte ought go without.

Helen felt the fight drain out of her. She felt tired and hungry and keen to go home. George was still musing on a way to withhold their allowance when Helen quietly quit the room.

'Is he to give us our money?'

Helen hesitated in the act of removing her hat and coat as her younger sister came into view. Wearily she shook her head.

Charlotte Kingston bit at her lower lip. 'He won't give us anything?'

It was whispered in a tiny trembling voice that immediately put the bellows to Helen's smouldering anger. Casting her outer garments on to a hall chair, she gave her sister a smile although her teeth were grinding. 'I think…hope he is considering how much he can afford,' she eventually said in a controlled voice. 'I have no doubt that he is embarrassed for funds: Iris was dressed from head to toe in new clothes. They looked French and expensive.'

'But it is *our* money!' Charlotte shrieked, pushing away from her sister's comforting embrace and stamping a small foot down. It made a hollow noise on the bare oak boards in the hallway of Westlea House. 'I cannot have new gloves, yet she has new gowns! How dare she dress in Paris finery at our expense!'

'She dares because our brother lets her,' Helen succinctly answered.

'George would never sell our home so he might settle with her dressmaker. It can't be *our* Westlea House that is advertised for sale in the *Gazette*…can it?'

Charlotte's nervous smile beseeched from Helen a reassurance, but she could not in honesty give it. Her bad news was conveyed in a hopeless shrug as she preceded Charlotte into the sitting room.

A meagre glow in the grate drew her towards the high mantelpiece. Absently she held out her palms to warm them, then looked around. Oh, she could see why her brother wanted to sell Westlea House. It might be spartanly furnished, and in need of some wallpaper and paint, but it was a fine-proportioned property, well situated on the outskirts of May-fair. Their neighbours included people who could boast an association with influence and aristocracy.

At one time, when their widowed papa had been alive, they had held just such a status, for Colonel Kingston was liked and respected by everyone with whom he came into contact. His friends included gentlemen of all classes: from peers of the realm to low-ranking army officers. It was through her father she had met Harry Marlowe. If Colonel Kingston was disappointed that his eldest daughter had chosen to accept a proposal from an army surgeon, who possessed little money but vast charm and kindness, he gave no indication. The marriage had taken place with his blessing, and a year later, when Harry was killed in action, his distress at losing his son-in-law had been genuine.

But her papa was no longer with them. He had succumbed to influenza within six months of Harry's death. At first their brother had scrupulously adhered to their father's arrangements for her and Charlotte. But then he had married Iris Granville and their lives had changed. Helen sighed and rubbed together her warmed fingers. She stepped to the window and looked out into the cold, bright afternoon. The baker's boy caught her eye as he hurried past, carrying a tempting looking parcel. Her stomach grumbled as she imagined what sort of wonderful aromatic treats might be wrapped within. She watched the lad cross the road and scamper down to the kitchen door of a house opposite theirs.

It would not have gone unnoticed by the other residents in

the Square that tradesmen rarely called at Westlea House. There was no doubt that their straitened circumstances were whispered over, and an embarrassment to some of their neighbours. Helen put up her chin and felt her pride rally. Those people might wish, as George did, that they would remove themselves to a humbler abode, but Charlotte and she were staying put, in the home in which they had grown up.

Charlotte *was* a beauty, Iris was right about that. Given the wherewithal and opportunity to socialise in the proper circles, she would doubtless attract suitors with vastly more to offer than poor Philip Goode could boast.

As though reading her mind, Charlotte whispered, 'If only Philip had some prospects, or an inheritance in the offing. Must I try and find a rich husband to help us?'

'Of course not,' Helen briskly said.

'If we must move out, where shall we go?' Charlotte asked in a quivering tone.

'Our fond brother thinks to move us to Rowan Walk.'

Charlotte's creamy complexion turned pink. 'That's where…where…certain women congregate…is it not?'

'Indeed…' Helen muttered. She chuckled. 'I implied Iris might make better use of it than us.'

Charlotte's eyes grew round. 'You did not dare!'

'Indeed I did!' Helen corrected with some asperity, 'And from the look that passed between them, I'd say that particular bit of gossip is true.'

'She is after Sir Jason Hunter this time?'

'Emily Beaumont said she made something of a fool of

herself chasing after him at the Pleasure Gardens.' Helen gave her sister a wry smile. 'Apparently he seemed more interested in bestowing his time on another lady, of rather dubious reputation, too. Mrs Tucker is quite lovely, though. I believe I have seen her once or twice in the shops.'

Charlotte looked scandalized. 'Poor George must feel so humiliated by it all.'

About to snap that their brother was a fool to tolerate his wife's behaviour, Helen simply shrugged. They had their own predicament to worry over. George showed them scant sympathy; let him deal with his own problems. And if, by the end of this week, their allowance had not arrived, she would add to his problems by returning to Salisbury Street to badger him again.

Chapter Two

'Give the lady a smile or she'll never go away.'

Sir Jason Hunter cast a withering look upon the gentleman who had made that ironic plea. He continued absently shuffling the pack of cards in his hands.

'Perhaps I ought invite her to join us. While she's fluttering her eyelashes at you she'll not be concentrating on the game in hand. I might relieve Mrs Kingston of a tidy sum this evening.'

Another quelling scowl met that teasing suggestion. Sir Jason did not appreciate his younger brother's drollery for two reasons: firstly, he didn't find Iris Kingston or her blatant interest in him attractive, and, secondly, his new mistress was becoming tiresome because she imagined she had a rival.

Mark Hunter lounged back in his chair and gave Iris a glance. 'She's pretty enough, and so desperately eager you'd be a fool not to put yourself at her service….'

Jason dropped the cards onto green baize and shoved himself back in his chair, boredom etched into his features. 'I need a drink,' he bluntly stated on gaining his feet. 'Have you seen Diana arrive?'

Mark retrieved the scattered cards with a swift sweep of a palm. He nodded towards a door that led out of Almack's gaming room and into the corridor. 'She flounced off that way some minutes ago. I'll wager she spotted your admirer before you did yourself.'

Jason jammed his hands in his pockets and blew an irritated sigh through his teeth. Nevertheless, he set off in the direction in which his sulking paramour was said to have disappeared.

As he passed a throng of females, that included Mrs Kingston, he was obliquely aware that fans were being feverishly employed and whispers becoming more urgently sibilant. Despite his reluctance to acknowledge them, his breeding impelled him to nod curtly, to nobody in particular, as he passed by.

About to quit the room, he noticed that George Kingston had propped himself against the wall and was moodily watching him. He and Kingston were known to be openly hostile; nevertheless, Jason diverted to where George was lounging—there was a matter of business that was on his mind. Following a perfunctory greeting, he launched straight away into, 'I understand you are looking for a buyer for Westlea House.'

George found a firmer stance and drew himself up in his shoes to try and equal his rival's height and breadth. Even with his chest fully expanded and his heels out of contact with the floor it was a futile task. 'I'm looking for the *right* buyer for Westlea House.'

'The right buyer or the right price?' Jason enquired, amused.

'What's it to you?' George snarled in response to that.

'I buy freeholds at the right price, as you know.'

Indeed he did know that, George thought sourly. The man he hated, the same man his wife was eager to bed, had a portfolio of the most prestigious addresses in major cities throughout England. Rumour had it he also now owned prime land abroad. 'A price named by you would never be the right price.' It was a poor bluff. If this man offered him what he wanted, he would sell to him, they both knew that.

Jason acknowledged George's petulance with a sardonic smile. It was no secret that the two men had once been friends, but now rarely spoke to one another. A roving glance told him that their conversation was indeed drawing some inquisitive looks.

Most people had assumed that, when Jason gained his title and wealth, George had resented being the underdog. But it was not inequality of status that had stirred such antipathy between them.

Despite their estrangement, Jason was a businessman, not too fastidious to ignore a prime opportunity if it presented itself. Once he had despised George, but the bitter incident that started it all had been mellowed by the passing of a decade. In an odd way, Jason felt pity that the man who once had been a good friend was saddled with a wife who acted like a harlot. It was not past enmity, but Iris Kingston and her pathetic ambition to be his mistress that would jeopardise any reconciliation between them. He returned to the business at hand and something niggling in his mind. 'I recall that your sisters reside at Westlea House…'

'Alternative arrangements for them have already been made,' George said quickly.

Jason nodded and, just for a moment, felt tempted to comfortingly grip his erstwhile friend by the shoulder and tell him that Iris would be wasting her time wanting a simple flirtation with him. But he knew such a sensitive fellow would construe any reassurance on the subject as effrontery. He glanced away to notice a woman he did desire in the doorway of the room. Diana was bobbing her head this way and that as though searching for someone. As her blue eyes alighted on him she instinctively flicked her blonde curls and struck a dignified pose. Jason's mouth tugged into a smile, for she had failed to convince him that she was careless of his presence.

'I expect we might agree on a figure.' He shoved away from the wall against which he had been propped.

George watched Jason saunter away. Inwardly he seethed at the cool confidence of the man, and the knowledge that, of course, he was right. He would sell to him.

'Shall we find some more interesting diversion?'

Diana felt a thrill shiver through her as firm fingers brushed her arm. She swung about in a whisper of pink muslin to glance coyly up into a pair of eyes the colour of gunmetal. She pouted and exaggeratedly glanced about. 'But, Jason, you might disappoint a certain person by leaving here so soon. Of course her husband would be delighted to see you go. He has a face like thunder.' The peevish note to her voice put Jason's teeth on edge. To subdue his sudden inclination to shrug and walk away, he allowed his gaze to linger on what about her was undeniably captivating.

Diana Tucker had a figure of exquisite proportions. She was of above average height for a woman, which suited him for he stood six feet tall. Her body had ample curves, yet retained a gracefulness that was often lacking in full-bodied females. She was blessed with a pretty face, too, and hair the colour of ripe wheat.

The stirring in his loins helped subdue his temper and he soothed her pique with a sensual stroke of a thumb. 'Come, there are better games to be had between us than those on offer here....'

Diana adopted a look of indecision simply to prolong his wooing touch. Alert to his impatience, she soon coyly lowered her lashes and voiced a breathy agreement to leave.

A few moments later, as Mrs Tucker swayed from the room on her lover's elegant arm, she made quite sure that Iris Kingston felt the full force of her bold-eyed triumph.

'Thank you, Betty.' Helen took the proffered letter and gave the serving maid a smile. Once the door had closed, she looked at the black script on the note's address for an indication from whence it came. 'It's from George,' Helen announced, then took another nibble at her breakfast toast before breaking the seal on the parchment. The toast, with so frugal an amount of butter spread on it, felt dry and scratchy in her mouth. Having moistened her throat with a sip of weak tea, she paraphrased, for Charlotte, the note's contents.

'It simply says that George would like me to visit today to discuss financial matters.' Helen sent a smile to Charlotte, who was seated opposite her at their small breakfast table. 'There! I knew he would come to his senses. He is ashamed at having squandered our funds on that selfish harridan he married.'

Charlotte picked up her tea and glumly watched the insipid liquid swirl in her cup. 'I think he has the devil of a cheek making you go there. He has a carriage and ought to come here. Why should you walk a mile or more to see him?'

Helen looked thoughtful at that. It would indeed have been more convenient for her brother to come to Westlea House than for her to be summoned to travel halfway across Mayfair. She shrugged. 'He probably thinks to make us work for our money. It doesn't matter; it is a clement morning and I like a walk….'

Helen handed her umbrella to George's servant, then carefully pushed back the drenched hood of her cloak. As she entered the small study in which her brother was lounging by the mantelpiece, she felt decidedly miffed. 'Really, George! Would it have hurt you to come to Westlea House? I expected you would do so once it came on to rain.' She shook out her damp skirts and heard one of her shoes squelch as she stepped towards the blazing fire to warm herself.

George frowned at the small puddle forming beneath the hem of his sister's skirt. 'Why in Heaven's name did you not hail a hackney in such weather?'

Helen raked her slender fingers through her sleek black hair whilst glowering at her brother. 'Would you have paid the fare when I arrived?' She gave a grim smile as she saw George's expression.

'Oh, I see, you have no money…I did not think…' George mumbled sheepishly.

'You never do,' his sister returned sourly.

George made a show of gallantly shifting away from the fire to usher Helen towards it.

'You will soon be dry,' he said cheerfully. 'A little bit of rain never hurt a person.'

'It is not a shower, but a downpour. If I catch a chill, I shall blame you,' Helen muttered as she removed her cloak and draped it on a chair-back to dry. Having made herself more comfortable, she turned expectantly towards her brother.

George shuffled uneasily beneath Helen's quizzical gaze. Abruptly he strode to the bell pull. 'Let's have some tea. I expect you could do with a nice hot drink.'

'I could rather do with our money. You do have a draft to give me, don't you?'

'Umm…not exactly…' George indicated that Helen should take a chair by the fire. 'But I have some…suggestions to put to you that might ease our problems.'

Helen cast on her brother a deeply sceptical look. 'What sort of suggestions?' she demanded. 'I have already said we have no more economies to make.'

'No…it is not that.' George passed a worrying hand over his jaw. 'In truth, I *would* have come to Westlea House, you know, but I do not want Charlotte to hear what I have to say.'

'Why ever not? She is nineteen. She is a woman in love…not a child.'

George nodded emphatically. 'It is this *woman in love* that is our problem. It is ridiculous for a girl with her charms to marry a man who can give her nothing when she could have so much.'

'It is as well that Charlotte is *not* in earshot!' Despite yearning that Charlotte be allowed to follow her heart, as she had, Helen understood the logic in George's words. Nothing was more certain to extinguish romantic love than relentless scrimping and scraping. Helen looked her brother squarely in the eye, hoping he was about to announce that he had managed to reinstate Charlotte's dowry. Briskly she said, 'Charlotte wants to marry Philip.'

'I have been thinking about Philip Goode and how he might perhaps improve his prospects.'

'And?' Helen asked eagerly.

'He is a cousin of Sir Jason Hunter, did you know that?'

Helen frowned her annoyance. 'No, I did not, but what is that to do with anything at all?'

'It is a very tenuous connection. A fourth or fifth cousin on his mother's side, I believe, is his kinship to Hunter.'

'This is ridiculous, George. What of it?'

'Jason Hunter is a rich and powerful man.'

'I hope you are not about to suggest that Philip goes to beg charity from his distant cousin. He is a man with pride and principles. He will refuse to do anything of the sort. But if you were to give Charlotte her dowry…even a lesser sum than the original, it would—'

George interrupted his sister by making an impatient noise. 'Any fund for a dowry will only come from the sale of West-lea House.'

Helen sent her brother a challenging look. 'Will you have a lawyer put that in writing? If I am to sacrifice my home, I will at the very least want to know that I have done so in order that Charlotte's future is secure.'

'A lawyer?' George exploded. 'Is my word on it not good enough?'

'Indeed it is not,' Helen said equably. 'Were you true to your word, we would not be having this conversation.'

'It is our sister's duty to find a man who can adequately provide for her. If she would socialise properly, she would attract gentlemen like bees to a honey pot.'

'She would also attract many cruel remarks. You know full well that she needs new clothes if she is to socialise in the circles you mean.'

'I'd get her gowns…if I didn't already owe a fortune to every blasted dressmaker in town.' George's features tightened in bitterness. 'None of those damnable things were bought to please *me*. Iris is attempting to impress Hunter with her new finery.'

Helen rose from her chair and approached George to comfortingly take one of his hands. It was the first time he had openly spoken of Iris's infatuation with Sir Jason Hunter. 'You must put a stop to her avarice. We are all suffering because of it.'

George snatched back his fingers. 'I don't need your pity, or your counsel. We must find a way of clearing my debts or Westlea House is to be sold. I have received some interest in it and cannot prevaricate for long.' George dragged a hand through his hair and snapped, 'For two pins I'd present Hunter with Iris's dressmakers' bills.'

Helen looked shocked, then a hysterical giggle erupted. 'Indeed, so would I if I thought he might pay them. But I've heard that he seems little interested in Iris.'

'Well, you've heard wrong, I tell you! He was flirting with her at Almack's earlier in the week. Anybody can tell that they're lovers.' George's face mottled with mortification for the untruth had easily burst out. He had noticed, as had every other person present that evening, that Jason Hunter barely acknowledged Iris. It had been oddly humiliating for him to witness his wife being shunned in favour of a demi-rep.

'Well, you ought to challenge him over it and take your dressmakers' bills with you!' Helen exclaimed in exasperation.

'I would not give him the satisfaction! I'm sure he flaunts their relationship simply to rile me. Why don't you speak to the arrogant bas—?' George snapped together his teeth before the abuse was fully out.

'Me?' Helen choked a shocked laugh.

George dismissed the subject with a terse flick of a hand and stalked off to glare through the window.

Helen was aware that her brother and Jason Hunter had fallen out many years ago. She had been about fifteen at the time of the estrangement and shielded by her papa from knowing the sordid details. But she had heard whispers that they had fought over a woman. At the time she had felt sad that Jason no longer visited, for she had liked him. More honestly she had harboured a juvenile *tendresse* for him. But now all that was inconsequential. Over a decade had passed and there were far more vital matters at stake than two grown men sulking over past slights.

'This is quite ridiculous.' Helen sighed. 'It is reprehensible of you not to have done your duty by us.'

'And it is reprehensible of you not to have done your duty by me!' George thundered. 'Do you think that I would have promised our father to support you had I known that seven years later you would still be a burden on me? Father was under the impression that, after a decent mourning for Marlowe, you would remarry, and so was I.'

Helen's face grew pallid. 'Papa didn't say that...'

'Indeed he did.' This time not a hint of shame betrayed the untruth that flew from George's mouth. 'He thought that by the time Charlotte had left the schoolroom, and was ready to make her début, you would have done the decent thing and removed yourself elsewhere. You accuse me of selfishness! You ought to look to your own behaviour.'

Helen stared, stricken, at her brother. 'Papa never mentioned anything of the sort to me,' she cried. 'I was always welcome in his house…'

'He probably thought he did not need to be blunt. He probably thought your conscience would guide you on it.'

George eyed his sister with calculation. 'Hunter wants Westlea House, he told me so at Almack's. I detest the man, but I shall sell it to him. I need cash quickly and he has a plentiful supply of the stuff.'

'You can't!' Helen emphatically shook her brother's arm.

'Indeed I can! Philip Goode ought to swallow his damnable pride and beg his cousin for assistance. Hunter has connections in the city. There are lucrative positions to be had in banking and so on.'

Helen stared at her brother, silently entreating him to reconsider.

'I can tell you think Goode too spineless a fellow to act. Believe me when I say Hunter is a different kettle of fish. He is a ruthless man and, once the deal is done, he would not hesitate in sending the bailiffs to evict you.'

Chapter Three

'**W**hat?'

Jason Hunter turned his grey eyes on his aged servant. He wasn't certain that he had correctly heard the message, for his visitors were creating a din that had smothered Cedric's croak.

The old fellow whispered again, 'A lady is here to see you, sir.'

'Yes, that much I gathered. What name did you say?'

Mark Hunter's second ribald anecdote caused the gentlemen congregating in Jason's library to resume guffawing.

'Mrs Kingston.'

Jason heard the husky sibilance through the noise and his mouth thinned before a low oath exploded through touching teeth. Enraged by the damnable audacity of the Kingston woman to bother him at home, he gave Cedric a curt nod and snapped, 'Put her in a side room and tell her to wait.'

Cedric dipped his wispy head, understanding exactly why his master was so put out. His weary bones might not allow him to venture far from the house these days, and his deaf ear might prevent him getting all the gossip, but he knew that a woman named Kingston was making a fool of herself over Sir Jason. Brazen hussy she was, too, with her haughty look. All airs and graces! He'd known her station straight away. Ask her to wait, indeed! It wouldn't have happened in the old master's days. Cedric wagged his head to himself. Oh, he'd find the baggage a place to wait!

'What was that all about?' Mark demanded as he watched Cedric slowly amble from the room.

'None of your business,' his brother rebuffed bluntly. He re-filled his glass from the decanter and asked Peter Wenham what price he wanted for his hunting lodge. The Wenham estate edged his own land at Thorne Park and the lodge and sur-rounding fields would be a fine addition to his Surrey acreage. A quizzical smile met the ambitious price his friend cited, but Jason gave that more charitable consideration than the ac-cursed female waiting for him below.

He would see Iris…eventually. But he'd let her kick her heels. Perhaps a little blatant incivility would finally penetrate her vanity; she might come to understand that, far from find ing her attractive, her behaviour disgusted him. If she could not take the hint, he would have to clearly tell her some truths. He was sick of being stalked and spied on when out; he cer-tainly did not intend having her hound him at home. If she re-peated to George what must, of necessity, be an unpleasant incident between them this afternoon, so be it.

* * *

One hour and five minutes later, when his brother and their friends had noisily departed, Jason descended the stairs of his opulent mansion in Grosvenor Square. He quite hoped his unwelcome visitor had tired of waiting for him and had removed herself. However, that would leave matters unresolved. He swore beneath his breath in exasperation. It would be as well if Mrs Kingston were still loitering about the place somewhere. Not by nature inhospitable, he nevertheless hoped that Cedric hadn't been plying her with refreshment to wile away the time. Within one step of the marble-flagged hallway he halted, and watched curiously as Cedric emerged, shaking his head, from a cloakroom.

Cedric glanced up and, seeing his master's bemused expression, hobbled across to glumly impart, 'I am afraid she has gone, sir. Mrs Kingston can't be found.'

'Did you think she might be lurking in there?'

The mildly amused comment caused Cedric's loose jowls to take on an unusual sanguinity.

Jason had hoped that Iris hadn't been mollycoddled; from his butler's guilty look it seemed he had little to fear on that score! 'Where exactly did you show her to wait?' he demanded to know.

Cedric's withered lips puckered mutinously on understanding the reprimand in Sir Jason's tone. He had been working for Hunters before this fellow was a twinkle in his sire's eye. He was the old master's servant, not this young pup's. Sir Gordon Hunter had been happy to leave the welcome…or otherwise…of uninvited callers to his discretion. Had Sir Gordon been alive, the Kingston woman wouldn't have put one foot over the threshold, let alone been given the courtesy of a seat. 'Bold as brass and looking at me with those cat's eyes…' he mumbled out defensively. A watchful, watery eye slanted at his employer. He had been subjected to that scowl before, and caught the sharp side of the fellow's tongue. Cedric now knew to quickly curb his insubordination, for he was aware the boy kept him on simply because his father had said he must.

'Cat's eyes?' Jason echoed exceedingly quietly.

'Eh?' Cedric cocked his good ear towards his master.

'You said she had cat's eyes.' Jason's tone held much volume and scant patience.

'Yellow…like a cat.' It was a statement accompanied by a wag of Cedric's head. He continued to mutter to himself. In his opinion he'd put the baggage where she belonged.

Jason frowned. He took little notice of Iris Kingston, avoided her when possible; nevertheless, he had been close enough at times to know her eyes were blue.

'What else can you recall of her appearance?'

'Thin…black hair…prim.' Cedric listed out each trait as though it was a sin.

Jason's eyes narrowed as he pondered on whom it could be the old fool had insulted. 'And she gave her name as Mrs Kingston?'

'Gave her name in full, she did. Mrs Margo May Kingston, she told me.'

The furrow in Jason's brow deepened. He knew no other Mrs Kingston. If for some bizarre reason an impostor were masquerading as the Mrs Kingston he did know, she surely would introduce herself correctly. Noticing that Cedric was sliding wary glances at him, he dismissed him with a flick of a hand and a caution. 'We'll speak further about this.'

As Cedric trudged away Jason took out his watch. Diana was expecting him to traipse around the warehouses with her this afternoon and he was already late. If his tardiness provoked a fit of the sulks he might be sorely tempted to go instead to White's and find some uncomplicated male company. He strode to the door, the question of his visitor's identity now submerged beneath thoughts of another exasperating female. At times he doubted Diana's delightful attributes were compensation enough for her juvenile nature.

'Please accompany me inside, Jason. How am I to know if you would rather see me in blue satin or lemon silk…?'

Jason felt tempted to honestly say that he couldn't care less in what Diana chose to garb herself. The only reason he paid for any woman's finery was to see it in a crumpled heap on the floor. 'If you can't decide between them, buy both.'

Diana showed her pleasure at his generosity by sliding along the phaeton's seat to rub her hip on his thigh.

Jason acknowledged the artful caress with a cynical twitch of the lips. He then tilted his head to watch a man beckoning him from across the street. 'I'll join you inside in a short while. Peter Wenham's over there and I want to speak to him on a matter of business.'

Diana limited her pique to a pretty pout. A most pleasing aspect of having hooked such a distinguished and wealthy protector was being able to show him off to envious females. There was no better place to parade her triumph than in Baldwin's Emporium, for women of every class were to be found browsing the sumptuous array of wares.

Diana's sulky expression brightened when she spied an acquaintance of her own. Mrs Bertram was approaching with a servant trotting behind. Obviously the woman had started shopping early, for the poor maid was bearing evidence of numerous purchases.

Georgina Bertram was the mistress of Lord Frobisher and an erstwhile playmate of Diana's. The two young women were of similar age and had been reared in rags in the shadow of the east London docks. Both had been blessed with abundant female charms and a most canny instinct on how to exploit such assets to escape the drudgery their mothers endured. They engaged in quite a good-natured rivalry when it came to finding rich gentlemen to keep them. With an affectionate squeeze for Jason's arm, Diana nimbly alighted, with a groom's help, from the smart phaeton. 'Don't be too long,' she breathily nagged over a coquettish shoulder. Soon she was entering the shop arm in arm with Mrs Bertram.

Jason sprang down from his high-flyer and, with an instruction for his groom to handle the horses, made to cross the road. He'd barely taken two paces when a rickety vehicle pelted past, far too close. He fell back against his phaeton, aiming a voluble string of oaths at the cab driver's head.

.The jarvey seemed unaffected by being so eloquently damned and, with barely a look at his victim, continued blithely on his way. Obliquely it registered in Jason's mind that a female passenger was within the contraption and that she seemed vaguely familiar. Suddenly she shifted closer to the window and from beneath a wide bonnet brim glared at him with large topaz eyes.

Helen sank back into the battered upholstery of the cab with her heart drumming wildly and a startled look on her face. She had not set eyes on Sir Jason Hunter for years, yet had recognised him instantly. Less than an hour ago the odious brute had snubbed her in an outrageous manner. He had allowed her into his house, then made her tarry in a cloakroom for an audience she was certain he had never intended bestowing. Hah! He'd been destined to see her after all! And be punished for treating her so abominably!

. Now that the shock of the close shave had passed, she allowed a throaty chuckle. *The Lord pays debts without money,* her papa used to quote when some misfortune was visited on a deserving recipient. Sir Jason Hunter might have escaped being flattened by her conveyance, but he certainly looked as though his dignity had taken a knock.

On rare sightings in the past she had exchanged a nod with Jason Hunter. A feud might exist between him and her brother, he might now be rich and important, but he was gentleman enough to be polite. Or so she had previously thought when appreciating his good manners. Now she knew differently. He had become an arrogant boor since last they had acknowledged one another. It was a pity his uncouth character didn't show in his appearance. She might have only had a brief look at him just now, but he was undeniably still a fine figure of a man. Suddenly a thought entered her head that made her squirm: she could understand why her sister-in-law was so smitten by him.

She quelled that thought by dwelling on the appalling incivility dealt to her less than an hour ago. When she had been shown to a seat in a cupboard filled with packing cases she had imagined that the butler had simply been confused, for he seemed a doddery old cove. When forty minutes later he put his head about the door and told her, with a crafty squint, that Sir Jason still wasn't ready to receive her, Helen came to the wounding conclusion that she was being intentionally insulted. She had quickly deduced that Sir Jason was spiting her because he hated her brother. With her head held high, she had swiftly exited the house without leaving a message of any sort with the footman who showed her out.

She had dredged up every ounce of courage she possessed to go and visit the swine. She had set out without a cogent plan, only hoping he would listen sympathetically to her family's predicament. She had considered requesting he delay buying their home, at least until her sister's marriage to Philip Goode could be arranged. To persuade him at that point she might have made much of the fact that the prospective bridegroom was one of his own kin. Such a squandered effort that would have been! She doubted such a man would care a fig for the nuptials of an impoverished distant cousin. It would have been better to set out this morning to again do battle with George, for this ridiculous situation could no longer continue.

Her brother might plead poverty and pretend to be an injured party but he lived well, far better than did Charlotte and she. He might not have ready cash, but he had assets to sell. The new landau in which his wife sashayed around town was just one such valuable item.

The cab drew up outside Westlea House and Helen handed over some coins to the jarvey. She gave his impassive wrinkled countenance a sharp look, wondering whether she ought to bring to his attention the fact that he had almost knocked down one of the *ton*'s most notable personages. She decided against it and, unusually, added a small tip to the fare.

Helen removed her grey velvet gown and carefully hung it on a hook. She had dressed with such care that morning in the few garments she possessed that were elegant, if dated in style. She had not wanted Sir Jason to see her looking like a waif and stray come abegging. A small smile twisted her lips; she might just as well have called on him dressed in her washed-out twill; all her painstaking *toilette* had been in vain.

Feeling chilled, she quickly donned her old day dress, then knotted a woollen shawl over it for warmth. She studied her reflection, lips tilting wryly at the incongruous sight of her faded blue gown hanging loosely from her slender hips whilst her hair was still primped to perfection. Briskly she removed the pins from her sleek coiffure and brushed through the silky coils. As she was about to loop it into a neat chignon, a loud noise startled her. She heard the doorknocker again being forcefully employed.

There was only one person she knew of who felt entitled to so imperiously announce himself: Mr Drover, of Drover's Wares and Provisions in Monmouth Street. Helen had been expecting him to call for a week or more. She felt sure she knew what the grocer wanted, and was tempted to pretend nobody was home. But that would simply delay the inevitable and deny them further supplies. With a sigh she quickly went below, her mind foraging for plausible excuses for delaying payment of what they owed whilst inveigling for another delivery soon.

'May I come in?'

Helen sensed her heart stop beating, then start to hammer in a rapid irregular rhythm. Obliquely she realised she had been terribly rude in instinctively pushing the door almost shut. She strove for self-control as she made wider the aperture by a few inches to blurt, 'What do you want, sir?'

Jason tilted his head to try and see more of the petite woman stationed behind peeling green paint. Merely a tantalising sliver of her figure was now visible and her features were concealed behind a curtain of loose dark hair. 'What do I want? I want to know what you want, Mrs Marlowe…apart from trying to assassinate me with a hackney cab….'

Helen jerked the door towards her and gazed at him with large astonished eyes. 'I did not intend you harm! It was an

accident! And had you been civil when I called on you earlier, you would by now know what I want.'

Jason found himself confronted by a fragile woman garbed
in a dress that looked as though it had seen far better
days…probably when it had fitted her. Now it was too large
and as shabby as the shawl she was gripping tightly about her
slender arms. His gaze returned to her face and lingered.
She'd been bonny as a child. Now a hungry look had pared
flesh from a heart-shaped face framed by hair as lustrous as
black silk. But it was her eyes that mesmerised him and he
realised that old Cedric's sight must be failing too if he
thought them yellow. They were the colour of fine cognac.

Helen felt herself flush beneath his silent, searing appraisal,
certain that she knew what prompted it. *He's wondering
whether I had the cheek to arrive at his grand house dressed
like this.* The thought brought slashes of colour to highlight
her sharp cheekbones and for a long moment she simply met
his slate-eyed gaze with haughty belligerence. Had he taken
the trouble to see her, he would not need to speculate on how
she'd been attired.

'May I come in?' Jason repeated. 'It might be as well to
have this conversation out of sight of prying eyes.'

Immediately Helen's gaze darted past him; it certainly
would give the neighbours something to gossip over should
she be seen trading accusations on her doorstep with a distinguished gentleman of the *ton*. For barely a moment longer
she dithered, undecided whether to send him away. But in
truth she knew she ought make some sort of explanation for

her unsolicited call on him. She also had been presented with a prime opportunity to do what she had really set out to do: to tell him that she and Charlotte were not willingly quitting their home, no matter what business he had hatched with her brother. Besides, now he was here, she had no intention of letting him go without taking a flea in his ear for treating her so vilely!

Helen crisply stepped back allowing him to enter the cold and gloomy interior of Westlea House.

In the parlour Helen indicated a chair by the unlit fire and then took the seat that faced it. She watched as Sir Jason Hunter perched his large frame, with effortless elegance, on the edge of the cracked hide.

After a tense moment in which Helen could think of nothing sensible to say because his eyes were so unnervingly fixed on her, she announced, 'I would offer you some refreshment, sir, but my serving maid is out at present.' It was true Betty was out; it was also true that only limp grouts, twice used already, were what she had to offer any visitor.

Jason moved a hand, dismissing the apology as unnecessary, then leaned back in his chair. From beneath subtle lids he considered Helen Marlowe and her intriguingly fragile beauty.

He had not spoken to her for ten years or so when he and her brother were still on good terms. He had heard she had married, and been widowed, but they no longer had any mutual friends who might bring them into proper contact. He racked his brain to try and recall the last occasion he had seen her at a distance and where that had been. He thought it had probably been in Hyde Park over two years ago. He wondered if she had then been as waif-like as she looked now.

Helen clasped her quivering fingers in her lap. She was sure she knew what he was thinking, for she was acutely aware of it, too: their status and social circles were now vastly different. Once he had been welcomed in to their home and she had been invited to Thorne Park to play with his sister, Beatrice.

Those past halcyon days were a world away from how she lived now. Now Charlotte and she socialised with people of their own station: people whose financial status limited their entertainment to simple at-homes. Outings to the theatre or exhibitions were treats that came rarely, for even the cost of travelling to such venues was beyond their means.

From the top of his glossy dark head to the toe of the gleaming leather boot in her line of vision, Sir Jason Hunter exuded an air of affluence and power that was stifling in its intensity. She had dared to go and see him, uninvited, to tell him he could not have this house. With wounding clarity she understood that, if he wanted it, he would take it. She raised her head and a flitting glance about her beloved, faded room encouraged her that he might decide Westlea House an unattractive investment after all. Her musings were brought abruptly to a close by a cultured baritone voice.

'I must apologise for the poor welcome you received when you called on me. My butler was confused as to your identity.'

'I'm not sure why,' Helen returned coolly. 'I gave my name.'

'What name did you give?' Jason asked. He leaned forward, linking his fingers and resting his forearms on his knees. He felt tempted to rub together his palms. The room was stone cold and a pale spring afternoon let little light into it. Nevertheless he could see her exquisite eyes watching him.

'I said I was Mrs Marlowe, née Kingston,' Helen answered him. 'I fail to see what is confusing in that.'

Jason's mouth took on a wry slant, for suddenly he understood how the sorry episode had come about. Helen Marlowe had a softly spoken, melodic quality to her voice. *Marlowe, née* had sounded to his deaf butler like Margo May. 'Cedric announced you as Mrs Kingston.'

'Why? Can he not hear?'

'Not very well,' Jason admitted with a ghost of a smile. 'Nevertheless, that is no excuse for his bizarre interpretation of my instruction to show my visitor to a side room. The incident won't go unpunished. I have long tolerated his eccentric ways. It is time, I think, to let him go.'

'I would not have you do that on my account,' Helen immediately objected. 'He looks to be an aged gentleman. I doubt he would get another position, especially if afflicted with poor hearing.' Helen knew too well the rigours of possessing little money; she didn't want it on her conscience that she had robbed an old man of his wages in his twilight years. She gave Jason a trenchant look. 'Besides, even if the draughty cloakroom was not your idea, I imagine the lengthy wait I endured was.'

Jason looked at the proud tilt to her sculpted little chin and felt utterly despicable to have subjected her to such discomfort and humiliation. 'I'm afraid it was,' he honestly said. 'And I am hoping that in some way I can make amends. I won't have you think I indulge in petty spitefulness because your brother and I don't see eye to eye.'

Helen met his gaze challengingly.

'That is what you think, isn't it?'

'It was,' Helen replied, 'until you clarified matters a moment ago.'

Jason's grey eyes narrowed on her. 'And what do you think now?'

'I think you believed my sister-in-law had paid you a visit. I think you decided to punish her by keeping her waiting for you. Why? Had you had a lovers' tiff?'

Chapter Four

'Lovers' tiff?'

The query was mildly quizzical, yet Jason's eyes resembled flint.

Helen felt her mouth become dry and her tongue trembled moisture to her lips. Moments ago he had said he would like to make amends for showing her such poor hospitality earlier that day. It was unexpected, but most welcome news. A favour from this man was *exactly* what she wanted, but ladies…even those of shabby gentility…did not speak of a gentleman's *amours*. Such impertinence was hardly likely to cultivate his goodwill.

Since Helen learned she had been mistaken for Iris Kingston a single thought had dominated her mind and she fervently wished she had curbed her inclination to voice it. Sir Jason had believed George's wife to be his visitor and his intention had been to eventually oblige her with his presence. Was Iris so besotted with the arrogant man that she would have allowed him to humble her in such a way?

Helen had good reason to dislike her sister-in-law, yet felt oddly piqued on her behalf. She was also a little indignant on her own account. How was she to know if, as Mrs Marlowe, she might have been turned away from his door?

The room was dim, his face in shadow; nevertheless, Helen winced on noticing a definite mocking slant to his lips. She feared he knew of her regret at having acted with such spontaneous vulgarity.

Iris had succeeded in her ambition to become his mistress. George had said they had been openly flirting earlier in the week…blatantly flaunting their affair. Such behaviour was sure to invite comment, thus Helen's face was beautifully prim as she announced, 'I am afraid I cannot pretend ignorance of your liaison with my sister-in-law. I have heard the rumours…' A hideous idea made her falter and demand, 'I hope you do not imagine I intentionally set out to impersonate Iris in the hope such a ruse would get me over your threshold.'

'Had you announced yourself simply as Mrs Marlowe, it would have guaranteed that you not only got over my threshold, but got my immediate attention.'

A cluck of disbelief dismissed that. 'You would not have known who on earth Mrs Marlowe was. When last we conversed, I was Miss Kingston.'

'Be assured, I would have known who you were.'

Helen's eyes darted to his at that husky affirmation. But still he made no remark about her impropriety. No doubt he considered it beneath his dignity to do so. But she could tell the matter had affected him. His composure could not completely camouflage that he was annoyed.

A tense silence ensued and Helen was conscious that he might now take himself off without questioning her further. Perhaps he had deduced from her attitude that she had gone to his house with the intention of interfering in his affairs. Sibling loyalty—however inappropriate—could conceivably propel her to confront the man who was making a cuckold of her brother. He had apologised and soothed his conscience, something she had yet to achieve for her own.

She was alert to a slight movement he made, sure it meant he was making ready to leave. 'I must say sorry, too,' Helen blurted. 'I was rude. I should not have been quite so explicit…that is…I accept that your association with George's wife is none of my concern. My brother is able to fight his own battles.'

'Is he? It occurs to me that perhaps he sent you to see me.'

Helen tensed at that observation and a surge of guilt stained her cheeks. It had indeed been her brother's angry challenge— whether uttered in jest or not—that had prompted her visit.

'Why would he do such a thing?' Helen flicked a nervous gesture. 'You would be hardly likely to pay attention to my opinion.'

'I'm doing so now….'

Tawny eyes sought to read his expression in the half-light. He had not sounded sarcastic, but it was hard to tell. 'If you are being sincere, sir, I must take advantage of the opportunity to…to…' She faltered, frowned at her fingers with the strain of being diplomatic. Her opinion, should she honestly give it, was hardly likely to be well received. How much attention would he want to pay to the fact that Charlotte and she endured hardship because his mistress was avaricious and selfish?

The loss of their allowance, and Charlotte's dowry, the imminent sale of Westlea House—all had come about since George took a gold-digger to wife. The thought that now she must petition the gold-digger's lover in order that she and her sister could have some basic necessities made ire burn in her blood. But she would not again make mention of the dratted woman. Rather she would concentrate on keeping her home.

'My brother is being dunned by his creditors and that is why he wants to sell this house. It is home to me and my sister Charlotte.'

Jason gained his feet in a lithe movement. 'And you have heard that I want to buy it.' It was a neutral statement.

'Yes,' Helen said, very conscious of the height and breadth of him as he passed her chair.

'You don't want me to have it?'

'It is rather that I do not want to lose it,' Helen said carefully.

Jason turned his back to the empty grate and cast up a glance at a ceiling meshed with cracks. 'I expect you will prefer living elsewhere. The upkeep of a property such as this is high.'

'It suits us to stay,' Helen interrupted firmly.

'George has arranged other accommodation for you and your sister, yet you'd rather stay here?'

'Indeed I would.' Helen breathed fiercely. So he knew that George wanted to locate them in a seedy neighbourhood. 'Our home might be rather shabby, but I am afraid even a flash house on Rowan Walk would be unacceptable. In fact, I have no intention of being dispatched there.'

Jason moved closer to the petite figure that had jumped to its feet. He could tell from her raised chin and tight fists that she was furiously embarrassed. And he understood why. 'Rowan Walk?' he echoed in disbelief. 'What the devil is he thinking of housing his sisters in such an area?'

'He is thinking of what he can afford,' Helen retorted immediately. 'I am sure he would have chosen somewhere more salubrious had his wife not squandered so much on gowns and hats and other selfish whims in order to hook you—' She abruptly bit at her lower lip to stem further angry complaints.

'Go on…' Jason quietly invited.

'Very well, I shall.' The declaration was child-like in its defiance. 'My brother is being dunned and I am to lose my home because your mistress is a selfish spendthrift. Whether you know it or not, sir, indirectly you are a reason we suffer.'

It was too late to perhaps phrase things more tactfully, but there was less volume to Helen's voice when she continued, 'George has dressmakers' accounts and so on that he simply cannot pay…'

'And I am to blame?'

'I have just said so.'

The impenitent statement elicited a mirthless laugh. 'You are a very loyal sister, if blinkered to your brother's faults.'

'On the contrary, I have no illusions as to George's character. He is weak and foolish to allow his wife to constantly manipulate and humiliate him. It is to my sister, Charlotte, that I owe my loyalty.' Helen moved closer to him, hoping the blaze in her eyes and the tenor of her voice would impress on him the strength of her outrage.

She looked into a face of raw-boned masculinity. Even as she glared at him, prepared to continue her tirade, she could not block the thought that he was breathtakingly handsome. 'You are aware that Westlea House has been owned by Kingstons for generations. It was Papa's intention that it should be home to Charlotte and me for years to come. Even had we both settled elsewhere with husbands, my father would have expected George to keep it in the family. He would be distraught to know his son married a shameless adulteress and, as a consequence, the house his wife loved must be sold for a paltry sum.'

'You think I intend to cheat you of its true worth?'

Helen was very aware of his grey gaze lowering to her face with that remark. 'You are a businessman, and very successful I have heard. I can't pretend to know much of commerce, but I'm sure you will want to negotiate terms favourable to you.'

'I'll pay a fair price for the property and George cannot withhold what is due to you and your sister from the proceeds.'

'We have no pecuniary claim on this house.' Tears of frustration sprung to Helen's eyes at that awful truth and she swiftly swung her face away. The movement caused black tresses to fly out and momentarily skim silkily on his dark hand. 'This property belongs in its entirety to George. We have nothing other than the memory of our father's wishes with which to bargain. Already George has broken his undertaking to dispense our allowance.' Helen turned to him, then held her breath as his eyes settled on her mouth. Abruptly she became aware of how close they now were. Barely a few inches separated her faded cambric bodice from the splendid wool of his jacket. She distanced herself with a small backwards step. And then took another.

In a moment of unguarded bitterness she had disclosed far too much that was private to a man she barely knew and certainly could not trust. He was her brother's enemy...hers, too, perhaps. It niggled at the back of her mind that he might use the intelligence she had just provided to his advantage. She might lack business acumen, but she understood the rudiments. It was extremely foolish to disclose one's desperation when negotiating a deal. Far from paying George what was fair for their property, perhaps she had just provided Jason Hunter with the ammunition he needed to haggle.

Helen sensed her spirit sapping. She felt like slumping into a chair to weep. She would not do that, of course, for Charlotte would fret to see her upset. Charlotte! She had forgotten about her sister's imminent return.

Should her sister come in and find her in the company of an imposing stranger, it would be certain to provoke a host of questions, the answers to which could only be depressing. 'I must ask you to leave, sir. My sister will soon be back from visiting her friends and…it is best no explanations are needed for your presence here.' Without awaiting a response to that, Helen walked, with confident step, to the parlour door and opened it.

Jason dipped his head slightly, ruefully accepting his dismissal. In the hallway he turned and stared significantly at wallpaper drooping loose close to the coving. 'You intend to stay here?'

'Indeed, I do.' Helen had bridled at his tacit disparagement. 'This property holds very happy memories of my parents and my childhood.'

Jason nodded absently, glancing about. 'I remember those days…I remember you…' Abruptly his eyes swerved back to her.

The look he gave her was lingering and penetrative and caused her again to blush. He remembered her… A decade ago her face and figure would have been attractively rounded by sufficient food. Her clothes would have been new and stylish. At fifteen she had been beautiful.

His quiet acceptance of her wretched appearance now was hard to bear. Had he displayed surprise or distaste at her deterioration she might have preferred it.

Having been in his company for some while without worrying unduly that she looked a fright, she was suddenly acutely self-conscious. She was ashamed of her worn dress and her locks wild about her shoulders. Belatedly she inwardly railed at fate. Why had he not arrived on her doorstep just five minutes sooner, when her hair was in its pins and she had been still garbed in her good clothes?

She jolted her mind from pointless wishes to say, 'I bid you good day, sir, and please take with you my apologies for the mishap on the road. The cab driver could not have seen you, I fear. Thankfully it seems no harm was done to you.'

A corner of his finely moulded mouth tilted, causing heat to return to her cheeks.

'I appreciate your concern, Mrs Marlowe.'

For some minutes after the front door had closed Helen remained staring at its paint-peeling panels with the sound of his softly mocking voice echoing in her ears.

'Mr and Mrs Kingston are about to dine, sir.' The manservant whispered that with a concerned frown. One didn't expect a caller at this hour, especially when it was a gentleman of such eminence. Robbins quickly deduced it must be a matter of some moment to bring Sir Jason Hunter here with an angry glitter in his eyes and his mouth clamped to a thin line.

Robbins had been in the Kingstons' employ long enough to know of the hostility that existed between this man and his master. He also knew that, whereas Mr Kingston didn't like Jason Hunter, Mrs Kingston did…rather too much, if gossip was to be believed. The idea that a pillar of polite society would flout etiquette and visit his mistress at her husband's house caused Robbins to almost snort his disbelief. He transformed the noise into a cough. 'Are you expected by Mr or Mrs Kingston, Sir Jason?'

'No, but I will not keep Mr Kingston long from his dinner. Please tell him that I should like to see him on a pressing matter of business.'

Robbins still seemed thoughtful and immovable.

'Tell him…' Jason urged gently, but a terse flick of his head betrayed his impatience.

The manservant needed no further prompting; quickly he hurried away.

'Have a care! Why are you haring about like that?' Iris snapped tetchily as she stepped from her bedroom to almost collide with Robbins.

Breathlessly the servant gabbled, 'There is a gentleman to see Mr Hunter…umm…I mean there is a gentleman to see Mr Kingston. Sir Jason Hunter is below.'

A wondrous look immediately lifted Iris's sulky countenance. So explicit was her excitement that it caused a sardonic twitch to her servant's lips. When the lady of the house inelegantly pushed past him to fly towards the top of the stairs, Robbins shook his head in disgust.

'Sir Jason…such an agreeable surprise…I hope…no, I must insist…you stay and dine with us.' It was coyly said and Iris posed with a white hand fondling the banister before swaying towards him in a whisper of sky blue silk. She kept her eyes lowered until close enough to coyly peep up at his face. What she read in his expression made a hand flutter to her pearly throat and a budding smile wither on her ruby lips.

'Thank you for your hospitality, but I am not here on a social call, madam. Where is your husband?'

Iris flinched from the ice in his voice, but was reluctant to relinquish the fantasy that he was really here to see her. His brusqueness she explained away: he was uncomfortable with her knowing he longed for her company. And Heaven only knew it was folly to visit her at home when gossip about them was already going around. When they were in public together he could appear aloof but that, too, was a simple ruse to camouflage his tumultuous feelings…a tumult she provoked! She was sure he would soon succumb to those secret yearnings and discreetly proposition her. After all, he could not possibly prefer that common baggage. *Mrs Tucker!* The harlot had never been wed! Diana simply sought to protect her worthless reputation by claiming the status of a widow and everybody knew it.

Iris smoothed her jewelled fingers over the shimmering silk of her skirt, pleased that she had chosen to wear it. She knew the colour matched her eyes and the snug fit to the bodice enhanced her bosom.

'What do you want, Hunter?'

George had been in his study and had just received his servant's breathless message that Sir Jason Hunter requested an audience. George's eyes narrowed suspiciously as he noticed how close together were his entranced wife and his unwanted caller.

'I want to speak to you,' Jason returned in a voice that was low and clipped. He stepped past Iris without giving her another glance.

'Can it not wait till tomorrow? We are about to dine.'

'Your wife has invited me to stay and join you. Shall I do that, or shall we attend to business so I might leave you in peace?'

Iris's lips tightened in annoyance for she knew full well George would rid them of Jason's company as soon as he could.

'Would you mind terribly leaving us, my dear?' George drawled the request, but a significant stare had Iris blushing. 'Ask Mrs Jones to delay dinner for a little while. This will not take long.'

After a twitched smile and a tiny bob Iris flounced away. Before disappearing below, she watched George show Jason to his study.

'What the devil is this about, Hunter? We were just about to sit down. Have you no notion of proper behaviour?'

'I was just about to ask you the same thing.'

'Me?' George choked an astonished laugh as he went to his desk and used the decanter. 'Well, just to impress on you that *I* am a gentleman with certain standards…would you care for a drink?' Without awaiting a reply he thrust a glass of brandy at Jason.

'*A gentleman with certain standards,*' Jason mimicked sarcastically. 'Why is it, then, you allow your sisters to exist in conditions more often found in Whitechapel than Mayfair?'

George gulped too quickly at his brandy and wheezed a

cough. 'Explain how you know... What do you mean?' he hoarsely corrected himself.

'This afternoon I went to Westlea House.'

George looked warily at him. 'You ought to have made an appointment for that. You had no right to go there uninvited.'

'You have sent me a contract to sign. I have every right to survey what I am buying.'

'Perhaps; but you have no right to study my family. How my sisters live is my business and none of your concern.' George sipped more sedately at his drink.

'Is that right?' Jason drawled. 'I've recently been told that not only is their plight my concern, but my fault. What is it you really want to sell me, George? Your house or your sister?'

Chapter Five

'That is an exceedingly strange thing to say. Am I to take it as a joke?' George frowned in studied thoughtfulness.

'If it were a joke, it would be in poor taste.'

'I'll take it as a joke, then,' George drawled with heavy irony. 'If I were to take it seriously, I should act as a good brother and defend Helen's honour.'

'How did you know to which sister I was referring?' Jason's teeth flashed in a silent laugh as George's complexion became ruddy. 'You've no need to answer.' His tone was husky with mock sympathy. 'Obviously I realise how you know, you sent Mrs Marlowe to see me.'

George snatched up his drink and took a swig before delivering a curt response. 'That is another exceedingly strange thing to say, Hunter, and not at all funny. It appears you have no notion of what is good taste.'

'It appears you have no notion of how to act as a good brother.'

George's mouth thinned. 'So you have this afternoon been talking to my sister Helen,' he snapped. 'What of it?'

'You sent her to see me. Why?'

'I did no such thing,' George angrily refuted. 'If you knew Helen better, you'd realise that she does as she pleases. A fine day it would be, and no mistake, if she followed my dictates.' He barked a laugh. 'If she did what *I* told her, she would by now be remarried.'

'And thus no financial burden on you.'

'Indeed,' George retorted without shame or remorse.

'I gather you were entrusted with the care of your sisters after Colonel Kingston died. Yet they seem to be fending, not very successfully, for themselves.'

'I'll not discuss any of my family's private business with you!' George thundered and slammed down his glass on a table that became beaded with brandy. 'How my sisters go on is none of your concern.'

'But you'd like to make it so. You're wasting your time, Kingston. If you have a clear conscience over it, I don't see why I should give a damn.' Even as the callous words were uttered Jason flexed the hand that remembered her touch. A phantom caress from ebony hair was again on his skin and a faint redolence of lavender water teased his senses. He cursed beneath his breath as fingers curled about the brandy George had given him. The amber spirit reminded him of the same soulful-eyed woman. Abruptly he put down the drink and walked to the door, aiming a contemptuous stare at George as he passed him. He halted with a hand gripping the handle.

'I've offered you a generous price for a property in need of extensive repair, and with tenants who are unwilling to leave.'

'There is no need for you to fret over my sisters' accommodation. I have already explained that I have made other arrangements for them.'

'And the dilapidations? The house has obviously been neglected for many years.'

George's mouth disappeared into a thin line. So that was what it was really all about! Money! Hunter had come to haggle over the price now he knew the condition of the property. George had expected to expediently conclude the sale confident that Jason would rely on a memory of Westlea House in its elegant heyday. 'Are you about to renege on the deal? If you have named a price beyond your means, please say so....'

'I think you know I have not,' Jason enunciated very quietly.

George fiddled nervously with the lawn knot at his throat, for Jason's icy grey gaze was unrelenting. He already regretted having resorted to using scorn. George knew, as did most people, that little was beyond this man's means. The knowledge was galling, yet he was wily enough to know when to retreat. 'Westlea House might now appear a little drab, but it is basically sound and will be grand again. When I have payment you will have vacant possession.'

'You think that your sisters will accept being moved to Rowan Walk?'

George made an exasperated gesture. 'I've had enough of this! You are being damned inquisitive and impertinent over matters that are not for discussion. You are not the only party interested in such a prime piece of property.' Smugly he crossed his arms over his chest. 'Bridgeman has made an offer on it.'

'But not at the figure I gave you. Nobody will match the sum, and you know it.'

George's smirk collapsed—his bluff had been immediately trumped. Colin Bridgeman's offer was far lower and George had been hoping nobody but he was aware of it.

George glowered at his adversary from beneath heavy lids. Hunter hadn't come here simply to complain that Westlea House was rundown. What was bothering him, George was sure, was his meeting with Helen. A crafty smile was imminent, but it withered as Jason stepped purposefully back into the room.

'Before I leave, it is timely to comment on some gossip whilst we are discussing family affairs. It seems your sister is under the impression that I am conducting an illicit relationship with your wife. She has heard a rumour, she said.'

George turned pale, but made no other indication that the subject affected him.

'I'm sorry to have to speak so bluntly, but this matter needs to be addressed,' Jason continued levelly. 'Let me make absolutely clear that I have no romantic interest in your wife. You and Mrs Kingston must deplore the nonsense that is being bandied about to the contrary.' Jason waited, but a rapid tic at the corner of George's compressed lips was all the response he received.

'There has been enough bad blood between us, George. I will not be falsely accused of a dalliance with your wife.'

George turned his back on his visitor. So! Helen had not minced her words with him. He now sensed that sly smile tug at his lips as he wondered whether she had gone so far as to demand he settle with Iris's confounded *modistes*. 'I'm surprised you think a mention needs to be made of it,' he slung over a disdainfully elevated shoulder. '*I* never comment on pathetic concoctions doing the rounds. What I will say is that my eldest sister at times forgets her breeding. She can be far too outspoken and act outside her role. I shall not apologise for her impertinence, if that is what you hoped.'

'You have no need to do so, Mrs Marlowe apologised on her own account.'

'When was that? When she called on you or when you paid a visit to her?'

George's tone held an insinuation that made Jason's eyes narrow to stony slits.

'I was otherwise engaged when your sister paid me a call. I was thus not able to speak to her until I surveyed the house.'

'I'm sure you took a thorough look at it all.'

'I always do when someone is too keen to sell me something.'

The threat George saw in Jason's countenance made him reconsider riling him further. He simply asked innocently, 'Are we to renegotiate the price because of the dilapidations you saw or the insults you heard?'

'I'll honour the sum first agreed on one condition: you find decent accommodation for your sisters.'

George examined his fingernails. 'What's it to you where they live?'

Indeed, Jason wryly thought, what was it to him? But the memory of Helen Marlowe's fragility cocooned by a threadbare dress was again in his mind. Despite her ugly clothing and unbound hair, despite her furious embarrassment when telling him she was to be sent to live on Rowan Walk, she had exuded a quiet pride…a stubborn grace. He recalled the feverish flush he had more than once brought to liven her marble-white complexion. There was meagre satisfaction in knowing that by discomfiting her he had momentarily kept her warm.

Helen Marlowe was neglected because her brother was weak and selfish and unable to control the grasping harlot he had married.

Jason wondered how Iris Kingston would like living in a freezing house, clothed in faded cotton. He wondered how she would withstand feeling hungry, for Helen had looked as though little nourishment passed her lips. He felt tempted to sneeringly voice his thoughts to her inept guardian. Instead he bit out glacially, 'I'll not have people think I'm in any way involved in putting two gentlewomen on Rowan Walk.'

'In case it's imagined you have a…shall we say, special interest in one of them? Both of them?'

Jason allowed that sneer to curl his lip. 'I've never yet housed a paramour so poorly. The fact that you would consider settling your sisters in such surroundings disgusts me.'

'I'm sure you know that your opinion of me counts for nought.'

Jason smiled his contempt on turning away. 'I'll let you get to your dinner…and your lady wife.' In the corridor he halted to say, 'Mrs Marlowe was alone when I visited. I didn't see your younger sister Charlotte. How old is she now?'

George looked startled at that question. 'Charlotte's nineteen. She's quite a beauty…'

'I'm sure,' Jason said drily. He enjoyed a leisurely moment before allaying George's anxiety. 'No need to fret, George, you chose the right one to send to me.'

George stared at the door for some moments after it had closed. He did not immediately go to the dining room to partake of his dinner. He returned to the decanter and poured another brandy. With a frowning countenance and a hand plunged deep into a pocket, he ambled to the fireplace to contemplate the smouldering embers. He tipped up his head to stare into a mirror soaring above the mantelpiece. A corner of his mouth lifted before a huge grin displayed his triumph. He raised his glass, saluted his reflection then downed the cognac in one swallow.

'He won't go, Mrs Marlowe,' Betty announced, with an air of resignation, from the parlour threshold.

Helen looked up from Mr Drover's account, hand delivered that very morning and accompanied by a terse, if ill-spelled, demand for payment for provisions delivered to date. Her eyes were fleetingly drawn back to the postscript in bold print: he would be back for payment before close of business today. Helen doubted it was an empty threat.

'Oh, for pity's sake!' Helen exclaimed in irritation. Pushing the papers away across the table, she jumped to her feet. She glanced over at Charlotte, who had raised her head from her embroidery on hearing her sister's vexed imprecation.

Bored with her stitching, Charlotte tossed the sampler aside and followed her sister into the hallway. Diversion, even of the variety that might conclude in unpleasantness, was a relief from monotony and hunger pangs.

Helen marched towards a grimy face cocked about her front door—it was the sum of the fellow she could see on her step. With a yank the door was fully opened and she looked fully at the mucky, pungent person. 'Look, my good man, my maid has already told you that we have not ordered a delivery. I'm afraid you are at the wrong house.'

'No, I ain't.'

'You are, I tell you!' Helen contested with strengthening volume and impatience. 'I do not even hold an account with your company.

'Bin paid for.'

'Well, in that case those…' a wagging finger indicated the coal sacks '…are most certainly not mine. Go to your depot and check your records.'

A blackened hand dived into a pocket and the coalman thrust a paper at Helen. A tantalising redolence of dusty warmth wafted to Helen's nostrils from his coarse fingers.

'Wot's that say?' he demanded.

Helen tilted back her head to focus on a scrawled address. 'There must be another Westlea House…'

'Not in this square, there ain't.' He tapped black dust on to the scrap of paper. 'That's what it says…see.'

A glimmer of an idea…extraordinary as it was…entered Helen's mind. She took the note and scanned it for clues. 'Did Mr Kingston arrange for this delivery and pay for it through his account?'

'Might 'ave bin 'im, but not on account. The yard clerk took cash.' A white slash appeared in his dusky complexion as he grinned. 'That's more'n good enough. No questions needed to be arst. Where d'ya want this put? I got other places to go, y'know.'

'Here is George now,' Charlotte whispered. 'He must have been feeling most generous. I expect he's come to make sure the coal has arrived.'

Helen looked from the merchant's surly countenance to the smart rig that had stopped behind a cart laden with oily-looking bags. 'So it is,' Helen muttered with an amazed little huff of a laugh. Never before had their brother taken it upon himself to order a stick of wood or a quarter of tea for them. Prising the money from him in order that she might do so was the routine they had invariably followed till now.

'I suppose there is a first time for everything. Heavens! I hope he has not come to ask for his money back,' Helen muttered, not wholly joking. 'He might have been in his cups when the guilty feelings took hold of him.' Stepping back from the door Helen instructed Betty to deal with the delivery while she and Charlotte went to the parlour to receive their brother.

George had barely stepped into the room, his hand hovering at his coat buttons, when Helen burst out, 'Why have you done such a stupid thing, George? You have paid cash? *Cash?*' she stressed angrily. 'Did it not occur to you that half of what you have spent on fuel might have been used for food? Do you think we might eat coal? And I am quite capable…as ever I have been…of ordering in my own supplies. I know what we need better than do you. Had you given the money to me, I would have used it far more wisely and—'

'What in God's name are you going on about?' George demanded. 'If you think that coalman is my doing, you are very much mistaken.'

Helen looked amazed, then distraught. As the consequences of what she had heard penetrated her mind, she dashed to the door. 'I knew it! It *is* the wrong house,' she muttered, appalled at the knowledge that the merchant would be in no mood to want to remove his wares from her bunker.

George caught at her arm as she made to fly past him. 'I doubt it is the wrong house and, if it is, it is that fellow's error, not yours.'

Helen saw in her brother's eyes a gleam of something akin to amused satisfaction. She was further convinced he was pleased with himself when he gave her a bright smile. Helen chewed at her lip. Past experience had taught her that it boded ill when George looked smug.

'Do you know more of this than you are letting on, George?'

George recommended unbuttoning his coat and seemed

about to shrug it off. As though suddenly conscious of the chill in the room, he pulled the woollen lapels together to cover his chest. Dropping his hat and gloves on to the table, he informed her with a slanting glance, 'Sir Jason Hunter came to see me earlier in the week.'

Helen felt her complexion heating beneath her brother's significant stare. Helen was aware of Charlotte's mystified frown at their brother's odd declaration. She had not mentioned to her sister anything about her meeting with Sir Jason. The opportunity to improve Philip's prospects had been forgotten and she felt rather guilty about that.

'Mr Goode and Miss Goode are arrived, ma'am.' Betty had again appeared in the doorway.

Charlotte immediately smiled shy pleasure at that news, unaware that her brother had muttered disparagingly beneath his breath on learning who were the visitors.

Helen was well aware that George had little time for Philip. On the few occasions they had come together at Westlea House in the past, George had made little effort to be friendly.

Once ushered into the room, Philip bowed courteously to the ladies, then immediately strode towards George and extended a hand. 'We have not met in some while, sir. It is good to see you.'

With scant enthusiasm in his greeting, George briefly shook hands before withdrawing and striding to take up position by the empty grate.

Undisturbed, Philip drew forward his sister, Anne, and introduced her to George. George managed an approximation of a bow to the plain young woman before drumming his fingers on the mantelshelf.

Anne Goode blinked rapidly, sensitive to the snub. Philip took his younger sister's arm and patted it into place on his sleeve, his smile still present.

Helen felt her temper rising at her brother's churlishness. Quickly she said, 'How nice to see you both. I had no idea you were to call by.' Helen slid a look at Charlotte to see her sister blush.

Philip might manage to appear impervious to George's moods, but he was unable to ignore his beloved's consternation. Quickly he said, 'Oh it was not arranged. Anne and I just thought to call and ask if you would like to take a ride. It is a sunny day and quite warm too.' He looked expectantly at Charlotte, who immediately gave a little nod. Gallantly Philip turned his attention to Helen. 'And you, Mrs Marlowe?

'I thank you, no,' Helen said. 'I have a few matters to attend to.' She gave her boorish brother a sharp glance. 'By all means get your coat and so on,' she told Charlotte. 'There is nothing much to keep you here this afternoon.'

Without further prompting, Charlotte quit the room.

Having watched her go, Philip cast a nervous glance at George. He suddenly took a deep, inspiriting breath and stepped away from his sister.

Helen drew Anne into a little chat, but was nevertheless more interested in hearing the intense speech to one side of her.

'I wonder if I might beg leave to visit, sir,' Philip began in a voice that shook slightly with emotion. 'For some time I have been meaning to come and see you on a matter that is very dear to my heart…'

George shoved away from the mantel against which he had been lounging and interrupted Philip in a voice that was cold and clipped. 'You can find me at my club, sir, most afternoons.'

This time Philip blushed to the roots of his fair hair at such an obvious rebuff. He managed a stiff bow before removing himself to hover close to the door. Within a moment Charlotte appeared. 'I am ready…shall we go?' she said quietly, having noticed from Philip's bright complexion that all was not well.

Once the trio had departed, leaving Helen and George alone, Helen rounded on her brother. 'I cannot believe that you acted so rudely.'

'And I cannot believe that the man has the effrontery to want to bother me at home to ask for my sister's hand in marriage. He has nothing. You only have to look at him to see that!' He barked a laugh. 'His shirt cuff! Did you see it? Frayed!'

'Like this, you mean?' Helen snapped and yanked down one of her own cotton sleeves for his inspection. 'Philip's sister cannot have offended you, yet you treated her with the same lack of manners.'

George tersely flicked away Helen's furious accusations and turned his back on her.

'I am ashamed of you, George. It is getting to the stage when I am loath to admit, even to myself, that we are related, for I am not sure that I like you.'

George pivoted back to glare at her. 'I do not want Charlotte seeing him any more. Make that clear to her or I will make it clear to him. And, as you have just noticed, I shall not stand on ceremony when I do so.' His face was livid when he added, 'I am sick of the burden of two ungrateful sisters to support. I will never countenance being saddled with a good-for-nothing brother-in-law, too.'

'I wish Charlotte had gained her majority and you no longer had power over her life.'

'She is nineteen and I am her guardian. She can do far better than marry him. In fact, perhaps she has already done so.'

'What do you mean by that?'

'I mean that I would hazard a guess that she has caught the eye of an extremely eligible gentleman. I would go so far as to say that it is to that particular wealthy gentleman you are obliged for that delivery of coal.'

Chapter Six

'You are talking in riddles, George. Charlotte knows no extremely eligible gentleman. We do not frequent places where she might meet such a person.'

'She has not needed to go anywhere. Recently a man came here, did he not?' On observing Helen's startled look, he added, 'There's no use in denying it, I've had the news firsthand.'

'Has Sir Jason Hunter asked you if he may propose to Charlotte?' Anticipating a dilatory response Helen came to her own scornful conclusion. 'I know he has not; but you'd like to make me think differently, wouldn't you? You might not like Philip, but this is truly absurd, George!' Helen's large golden eyes demanded a retraction from him, but a smug look was all she received. Helen sighed disappointedly. 'Apart from the fact that a delivery of coal would be an extremely odd courtship gesture, Jason Hunter did not even see Charlotte earlier in the week. She was not at home when he called.'

'I know she was not here. He mentioned that he missed seeing her…amongst other things.'

Helen stared at her brother, perplexity arching her dark brows. 'What exactly did he say?'

'That you were rude to him.'

'I was not!' she spluttered, but with guilty spots of colour seeping into her cheeks. 'I simply told him some truths, and you cannot deny you didn't want me to!' She felt depressed from knowing Jason Hunter had immediately tittle-tattled about her to George. She had not believed him to be that sort of mean character. 'In any case, it ill behoves a libertine to preach about good manners.'

'Never mind about that now,' George airily dismissed. 'Whatever you said, I think it might have had a most beneficial result. Hunter came to see me within a short while of leaving here. He spoke of Charlotte in a way that makes me certain he finds our little sister…interesting.'

'What did he say?' Helen demanded.

'I recall a mention was made of her beauty…' It was a statement calculated by George to imply that the compliment had not been his. Briskly he continued, 'Hunter made a point of asking her age. It is as well Charlotte has gone out for I wanted to speak to you in private. Do you think that he has recently spied her out walking with friends and taken a liking to her?' George subdued a smile on noticing his sister's deep concentration. 'It might end in a family feud if Hunter takes her on. But at least Goode would be saved the indignity of going cap in hand to his cousin.'

'Oh, be quiet, George!' Helen exploded, unimpressed by her brother's drollery. 'Now I think sensibly on it, I see it is just another deluded fancy of yours, concocted in the hope of securing someone rich to clear your debts. None of it alters the fact that Charlotte loves Philip.'

'And Hunter won't give a damn either way.' George bestowed on his sister an extremely patronising smile. 'I realise you were not married long, Helen; perhaps that explains why you often seem too naïve.'

A suspicion of to what her brother was alluding made Helen's soft lips slacken in disbelief.

'Jason won't countenance getting leg-shackled to a woman with nothing to offer but her looks.' George snorted a coarse laugh. 'I know of several ambitious chits with good dowries who would forgo being a duke's wife to marry that particular baronet. He's planning to use his cash to lure a high-born filly and found a dynasty.'

Alarm and anger vied for precedence in Helen's mind now she clearly understood what her brother meant. If Jason Hunter wanted to buy his heirs a nobler lineage, so be it. She was not interested in his aspirations. But the prospect of her sister's ruination was very much a concern close to her heart.

For a few fraught moments Helen played over in her mind all that had passed between Jason Hunter and her when he had come to Westlea House. Had she been so obsessed with lambasting him over his relationship with Iris that she had missed vital clues that he was preying on someone far dearer to her? Her conclusion was that there had been no word or deed of his to make her suspect him a callous seducer of innocents. When she had asked him to leave because Charlotte would soon be home he had not attempted to find an excuse to loiter, and surely he would have done so if he were attracted to their young sister.

With shocking and depressing insight she realised it was not Jason Hunter she mistrusted, but her own brother. 'I cannot believe you would accuse a gentleman of being capable of anything so despicable!' She glared at George, but he simply returned her an impenitent smile. 'Sir Jason might have a reputation as a rake, but I'm certain he leaves maids alone.'

Helen's mounting outrage had made her slender body tense as a spring and her censure increasingly vociferous. In fact, so absorbed had she been in railing at George that for a moment she was unaware that his attention was riveted elsewhere.

What wounded Helen most was the knowledge that their brother—the person their father had trusted would protect and care for his sisters—considered Charlotte's degradation would be a *surprisingly beneficial result* to recent dealings with Jason Hunter.

Helen whipped about to face her brother and was momentarily struck dumb. Betty was, once more, hovering awkwardly on the parlour's threshold, her red countenance bearing testament to her having overheard rather too much of the contretemps between sister and brother.

'There is a gentleman caller, Mrs Marlowe,' Betty announced in a croak, her eyes gliding to the side to indicate the hallway.

Obviously the visitor had also heard Mrs Marlowe shouting like a fishwife. Helen took a steadying breath and submerged her regrets at having been caught out in such unladylike passion, beneath a soaring optimism. She offered up a silent prayer that Samuel Drover had returned to collect his payment and was in no mood to be fobbed off. Fervently she wished the grocer might today succeed in cornering George into settling his account.

But Betty's next whispered words withered any such hope and sent icy fingers to momentarily squeeze still Helen's racing heart.

'The visitor…umm…he…it's…Sir Jason Hunter, ma'am,' Betty concluded.

Helen felt a strange mix of dread and defensiveness coiling cramps in her stomach. It was possible Sir Jason had not heard his name mentioned, or discerned the nature of their heated exchange. But certainly he had heard her sounding like a raucous harpy. She darted a glance at George; his expression betrayed a peculiar ruefulness. Jerking her faculties into action, Helen tilted up her chin and instructed clearly, 'Please show him in, Betty.'

'So, you think my theory absurd, do you? I wonder what brings him here?' George peered closely at Helen. 'Try and make yourself presentable, for Heaven's sake. You have dirt on your cheek. Hunter will think you a slattern.'

Helen's fingers spontaneously jumped towards her face. She gave a tut of dismay as she noticed that the very digits she had been about to employ to remove the spot bore evidence that they had caused it. It was likely the dust had come from the scrap of paper the coalman had given her.

Quickly she wiped her stained fingers on her skirt just as she heard George announce, 'Hunter, fancy seeing you here....'

'A pleasant surprise, I'm sure....'

It was a wry retaliation to her brother's sarcasm and made Helen wince. She raised watchful eyes to Jason's face and again marvelled at features that were both ruggedly masculine yet finely proportioned.

Perhaps aware of her regard, he turned to look at her. Helen proudly tilted her chin and quickly clasped her mucky hands behind her back.

If he was aware that he'd figured in the argument he'd overheard he gave no outward indication. He looked no less cool and composed than he had when last she had seen his sartorially splendid physique stationed in her shabby parlour. And she looked...only slightly better than she had on that occasion, she realised. The bulk of her thick hair was still in a chignon, and her serviceable brown skirt and crisp cotton bodice were an improvement on her faded blue cambric. But on that previous occasion at least her face had been clean. Whilst the two men exchanged a few words Helen casually brought the cuff of a sleeve to her cheek and scrubbed. Her hand dropped back to her side as she heard her name spoken in a husky male voice.

'I trust I've not called at an inconvenient time, Mrs Marlowe.'

It sounded innocent enough, but there was a gleam of amusement in his grey eyes letting Helen know the nicety was ironic. Blood fizzed beneath her skin, but instinctively she sketched a bob in response to his greeting. 'Unfortunately you have, sir,' she boldly told him. 'My brother and I were in the middle of discussing some important domestic issues. I'm sorry to seem inhospitable, but—'

'Helen! Where are your manners?' George interrupted with a reproachful tone and an easy smile. 'There is nothing we were talking about that can't wait for another time.' Pulling out a heavy gold watch, he consulted it with a regretful sigh. 'Look at the time! Much as I would like to tarry and be sociable, I must be on my way. My attorney is expecting me to call on him in Cheapside and after that I have to attend to pressing business in Holborn. Why do you not get Betty to fetch some tea, Helen? I expect Charlotte might soon be back and join you.' He sauntered to collect his hat and gloves from the table before carrying on towards the door.

'Perhaps Sir Jason might think *you* rather impolite,' Helen sharply addressed her brother's back. 'Will you not stay just a short while, George, and keep us company?'

'Of course I should like to, but I'm late already. Besides, I doubt Jason is come to see me. Anything in particular you must say to me, old chap?' he asked with affable charm.

'Not a thing.'

There was again an inflection to her visitor's tone that made Helen sure the two men were tilting at one another. But her overriding desire was to get her brother to tarry long enough to give her an opportunity to slip away and tidy her appearance.

Having come and violently upset her, George was going to insouciantly depart and leave her to deal with the awkwardness of Jason Hunter's untimely arrival. The slippery devil was also going to avoid a confrontation with Mr Drover this afternoon. George was once more about to wriggle free of providing the wherewithal for some provisions.

For some moments after George's slick departure from Westlea House, the only sound in the cool parlour was the rhythmic tick of the mantel clock. Helen managed to subdue her anger at her sly brother for long enough to remember to offer what meagre hospitality was available. 'Please do sit down if you wish, sir.'

Whilst her visitor was seating himself on the ancient leather chair he had used once before, Helen was finding another reason to despise George. His blithe assumption that she had refreshment to give a guest was a typical example of his careless ignorance over how his sisters existed at Westlea House.

Suddenly she pounced on a useful memory. In the dining room was a decanter half-full of Madeira. George kept it replenished in case he fancied a tipple when dropping in on them. Conscious of grey eyes steadily observing her profile, Helen announced with the aplomb of a competent hostess, 'If you would like a drink, sir, my maid will be pleased to fetch you a glass of wine…'

'I thank you, no,' Jason said with a crooked smile. 'I shall endeavour not to outstay my welcome.'

Helen again felt blood tingle beneath her cheeks. Perhaps his voice held no humour and she was simply too sensitive to being mocked.

She resisted the urge to press her fingertips to her face where skin felt singed by eyes like charcoal embers. She knew he had noticed the smudges on her face and the knowledge irked enough to make her prickly. 'Is there a reason for your visit, sir?'

'Indeed there is. I have come to advise you that I have arranged for a load of fuel to be delivered. Has the coalman already been? You look a little sooty…'

Helen inwardly winced, but nevertheless brought her mucky fingers into view and wiped them, very deliberately, with a handkerchief whipped from a pocket. 'As you can see, sir, the delivery has indeed just arrived and, being unexpected, was inconvenient.' She rolled the stained cloth into a ball and hid it in a fist. 'Whilst not wanting to look a gift horse in the mouth, perhaps you would care to explain why you thought to interfere in something that is not your concern.'

'But it is my concern, Mrs Marlowe,' he softly corrected. He leaned back in his chair, lifting a boot to settle at an angle on the other leg. His long lashes screened the expression in his eyes as he said, 'Maintaining this house is now my responsibility. The structure is damp and I have decided it would benefit from some warmth in the rooms.'

Slowly Helen absorbed the awful significance of what she had heard. 'Westlea House is now your property?'

'Yes.'

'The deal is all done? It is finalised so soon?' Her voice was little more than a horrified whisper. As though the full force of the news had finally penetrated, Helen allowed a startled glance to flit about the parlour, as if trying to imprint every faded feature on her mind.

'The sale was finalised a few days ago. I'm surprised that your brother has not already found an opportunity to tell you of it.' Jason paused, looking thoughtful. 'Has George said anything at all to you about the terms and conditions we agreed?'

Helen absently shook her head. She cared little for knowing the details of the deal. Besides, she could guess that the terms and conditions to which he referred centred on the speedy ejection from the premises of George's sisters.

Suddenly she perceived exactly why her brother had been so eager to immediately leave when this man arrived. George had cravenly scampered away lest the news slip out and cause a bad atmosphere. He would not like his sister to harangue him, in front of such an influential acquaintance, over the indecently hasty sale of their childhood home. Helen grimly realised that, had her brother been still within range, she might have forgone a verbal assault in favour of a physical one. Her fingers unconsciously wrung the handkerchief until it loudly yielded. She looked down at the shredded linen, then carefully put it out of sight in a pocket.

It was useless blaming Jason Hunter for depriving her of her beloved Westlea House. It was all George's fault. She walked in a daze to the window and gazed out sightlessly at

a smart phaeton. Her trancelike state prevented her from noticing that a neighbour out walking had hesitated to peer in-
quisitively between the expensive equipage and her front
door. Suddenly Helen whirled about to launch some breathless questions. 'Must we leave here immediately? Is that the
real reason you have come today? To give us notice to quit?'

Having accepted the comfort of a chair for barely a few
minutes, Jason was again on his feet. He shoved his hands in
his pockets and, tipping up his head, frowned at the ceiling.
'No, that is not the reason I came here, Mrs Marlowe. I was
actually speaking the truth when I said I wanted to tell you a
merchant would be calling.'

Helen flushed beneath the tacit warning that he resented the
implication he was a liar. But she was to anguished by the loss
of Westlea House to offer an apology. All she would now deal
in were hard facts. 'When must we leave?' she demanded to
know, struggling to sound coolly polite.

'You may stay here until your brother finds you suitable accommodation.'

Helen smothered a laugh with the back of a quivering hand.
'You must be a patient man then, Sir Jason, for I will never
find Rowan Walk suitable.'

'Then George must rent another property. If he fails to do
so, he will forfeit a sum of money. It is a condition of the sale,
signed and witnessed, that you and your sister are housed
somewhere that is acceptable to you.'

Helen's fists tightened at her sides. 'And that condition was
your idea?'

Jason signalled a brief affirmative with a lazy hand and an expressive lift of his dark brows.

'If you are expecting me to thank you, sir, I am afraid I cannot. If you withhold George's money, he will use that as an excuse to continue to keep us short. Besides, *this* house is the one acceptable to us.'

'If it is really what you want, you may stay here.'

Helen's topaz eyes flew wide in astonishment. A moment later they had narrowed suspiciously. George's theory on this man's interest in Charlotte niggled mercilessly at her mind. Gentlemen did not offer shelter to young ladies unless they were relations…or the target of lustful intentions. 'What do you mean…we may stay here?' she enquired in a glacial tone.

'I mean that your brother must rent you somewhere to live. This house is now mine and I would consider granting a tenancy on it.'

'You would not when you discover how little my brother would be prepared to pay you,' Helen said with a brittle laugh. 'The property on Rowan Walk is taken for six months and he will not squander the expense of that. I told you he had committed to it when last we met. Perhaps you had forgotten what I said.'

'I haven't forgotten one thing you said to me, Mrs Marlowe. And, I repeat, if you want to remain here, I'm sure something can be arranged.'

Helen again felt an alarming *frisson* race through her. Had she misjudged and berated George unfairly? Her brother might think her too naïve, but unbeknown to him she had personal experience of the negotiations between rich men and poor women.

Two years ago she had received, and rebuffed, a proposition from a gentleman wanting to offer her his protection. Colin Bridgeman had written to her of his respectful admiration and of how he was confident that *something could be arranged* between them. Helen had felt at the time quite angry when Mr Bridgeman had ignored her curt note of refusal and written again, coaxingly, of the benefits she would receive. She had been on the point of telling George to speak to the insufferable lecher. Now, of course, she was glad she had kept the matter private—doubtless George would have insisted that she take up Mr Bridgeman's kind offer.

Helen shot a wary glance at Jason's face. He returned her regard with quite pleasant directness.

She had spoken to him once before in a blunt way that would guarantee her ostracism by polite society should they ever know of it. Taking a deep, inspiriting breath Helen blurted out, 'I must beg your pardon, sir, and your forbearance, but I find I must again speak to you in a way that will be considered shockingly improper.'

'Please say what you must. I'd rather there was no misunderstanding between us.'

But having boldly got that far, even his gentle prompting could not bolster her courage. Looking up at his worryingly handsome face, she decided first to try and prise some clues from him. 'When you arrived here today…I expect you overheard…that is…I'm sure you know George and I were arguing.' Large amber eyes peeked up through a web of inky lashes to discern his reaction.

'I admit I was aware of a heated exchange.' Jason's mouth tilted, but he seemed unwilling to elaborate.

'I'm not sure how much you overheard…' Helen probed.

Jason felt tempted to smooth back the lustrous strand of hair that clung stubbornly to her soot-smudged cheek. Instead he murmured, 'Please don't embarrass yourself by mentioning it further, Mrs Marlowe. Suffice to say that I was not disappointed on hearing your opinion of me.'

Helen felt fiery blood rush beneath her complexion.

Seeing he had heightened her confusion, Jason soothed softly, 'My intention was *not* to embarrass you, Mrs Marlowe. Let's say no more of it.'

Helen cleared her throat. 'I find I cannot just dismiss it, sir, for I'm not now sure that George deserved the ticking off I gave him.'

'And what has changed your mind?'

'Something you have said…'

Jason twisted a slight smile. 'Ah, I see. You no longer think me a principled rake…just a rake. Will you enlighten me as to how I have disgraced myself in such a short while?'

Helen nodded, but his mild mockery had made words again awkwardly clutter her throat.

Jason walked to the cold marble mantel and braced a lean hand against it. 'Let me hazard a guess and save you the ordeal of telling me. You think that any benefits I have offered will be subject to unpleasant conditions. Let me reassure you.

I do not need to coerce widows in straitened circumstances into sleeping with me.'

Helen's beautiful eyes shot to his face as the awful truth registered. He thought she was hinting he found *her* attractive.

'Me?' Helen gasped in a voice that hovered between ridicule and outrage. 'Oh, no! I don't think you want me at all. I think it is Charlotte you're after.'

Chapter Seven

'Charlotte? Your younger sister?'

Helen had to admit that his astonishment seemed genuine. His brow, visible beneath a fall of dark hair, had furrowed, and he looked ready to laugh. Feeling unaccountably nettled by his reaction, she gave a curt nod.

'You think that I have designs on your sister's virtue.' It was a toneless statement and he now looked far from amused.

Helen felt her pique wilt beneath his latent anger. She chewed nervously at her lower lip and tried to avoid the ominous glitter in his eyes. But still she wanted to hear his denial. 'Are you saying you didn't intend to attach strings to your generosity?'

'Is there any point in saying anything at all? It seems I've already been found guilty as charged.'

'No! That's not true. I told George I did not think you capable of callously seducing a chaste young woman.' She had come closer to him in her agitation and a small hand raised as though she would clasp his forearm in emphasis.

Just for an instant their eyes coupled, travelled together to her outstretched fingers. Helen quickly curled the slender digits into her palm and the fist dropped to her side.

'But you think my leniency extends only to untried maids,' he stated quietly.

'I do not think you a callous man at all,' Helen briskly said with a crisp back-step. 'I'm sorry if I have offended you, but I did warn you I had nothing pleasant to say. Charlotte is just nineteen and hoping soon to get engaged. A hint of scandal would ruin her reputation and her future.' She hoped that her apologetic explanation had sweetened his temper, but received no such sign.

A finger fiddled a bothersome curl behind a small ear. 'I'm sorry I mentioned any of it. It is just that…someone said you were showing an unusual interest in Charlotte.'

'I wonder who it was?'

The question was soft, sardonic, and Helen knew that trying to shield George was pointless. Jason was perfectly aware who had sown that particular poisonous seed in her mind.

The best form of defence is attack, her papa would have counselled had he known her predicament. And she did have a grievance of her own to air! 'I know you went to see my brother after you left here last week. He told me so this afternoon.' She gave him a reproachful look. 'I had already apologised to you for being impertinent that day. Perhaps if you had not gone off telling tales to him my sister's name would not have arisen and thus no misunderstandings either.'

'So I'm not only suspected of being a brute, but a tattler, too.'

Jason shoved his hands deep into his pockets and slanted a searing look at her from beneath curved black lashes. 'Do you seriously think I would waste an hour of my time bleating to your brother about how horrid you had been to me?'

Helen winced at the dark irony in his voice. 'I realise you had other matters to discuss with George, too,' she tartly allowed.

'Indeed, I did,' Jason drawled. 'Actually, I must thank you, Mrs Marlowe, for bringing something to my attention. It seems that a comment from me was long overdue on a slanderous rumour going around. I have not cuckolded your brother and have no intention of doing so.'

Helen's heart jumped a beat, then started an erratic tattoo beneath her ribs. She had certainly not expected *that* to be one of the topics he had discussed with George. 'Be that as it may, sir,' she breathed, 'you have only yourself to blame that people have assumed differently. If you flirt outrageously with my sister-in-law, you ought know gossip will ensue.'

'I abandoned flirting a decade or more ago, Mrs Marlowe. And you ought know that, where I am concerned, your brother is a regular mischief-maker. I suspect his wife is, too.'

He was correct, of course, in his assessment of her kin. Moreover, she believed he had been wrongly maligned, and thus could have made much more of a complaint than a taciturn observation on the devious natures of her brother and sister-in-law. Nevertheless, Helen instinctively bristled at receiving even a mild rebuke from him. She blinked and moistened her dry mouth by delicately tracing her lower lip with her tongue tip.

His steady, penetrating appraisal flustered Helen and she fought to equal his calm demeanour. She wished he would go, yet, confusingly, was reluctant to lose his company. There was something about him that was daunting, yet very appealing. He seemed in no rush to leave despite having done his duty and advised her of the coal delivery. Perhaps he was allowing her an opportunity to raise objections to his criticism of George and Iris from consanguinity. But her selfish sister-in-law deserved no such championship, and she baulked at the level of hypocrisy required to defend her brother.

Unspoken words seemed to whisper between them in the tense silence. She sensed he was daring her to voice the thoughts haunting her mind. Persistent phrases crept again to teeter on her tongue-tip. *Why do you stare? Is it me you want?*

Helen compressed her shapely lips into a tight line as though forcibly preventing any such shameful utterances from escaping. Jason Hunter had told her earlier, with faint scorn, that he had no need to coerce widows in straitened circumstances into sleeping with him. But what if they needed no such persuasion?

Helen averted her face, hoping to conceal the blush she again felt staining her complexion. It was not his potent presence that caused her embarrassment, but her own unquiet mind. She had never before considered herself conceited, yet a silly fantasy that this gentleman might desire her would not quit her thoughts.

Helen knew, as did the rest of polite society, that Jason Hunter had selected Mrs Tucker to fill the role her sister-in-law coveted.

Some months ago, when she had been out walking with Charlotte and a friend of theirs, Emily Beaumont, she had observed a beautiful young woman alight gracefully from a shiny carriage drawn by a pair of splendid greys. Servants in smart black livery had been in attendance and the ensemble had drawn admiring glances, not only from Helen's party, but from other people promenading, too. Emily had whispered that Sir Jason Hunter had provided the lady's transport. It was at that point that Helen learned from Emily the identity of the favoured lady and why Sir Jason would be so generous.

Diana Tucker had soon made her way, with confident step, into a shop. Helen had pensively studied her stylish outfit, thinking that, with her superior air and elegant bearing, she might have been a nobleman's daughter rather than a notorious courtesan.

In her mind's eye Helen could again see blonde curls dancing over blue velvet shoulders and a pretty face shadowed by a plumed hat cocked to a jaunty angle. In her nostrils was a faint redolence of an exotic perfume that had wafted in Mrs Tucker's wake on that particular afternoon.

An involuntary glance down at her appearance took in her drab skirt and frayed cuffs. Her critical eyes spotted the soot smudges on her hands and she absently rubbed her fingertips together. She recalled that her face was similarly grubby and her hair dishevelled. At that moment she was conscious of how very risible was her idea that she might attract a disturbingly rich and handsome baronet. It prompted her to stutter into the silence, 'For…forgive me, sir, but it seems we have said all we must. My sister will soon be home, and…'

'And you would like me to leave,' he finished for her in a wry tone.

Helen nodded and managed a grateful smile. She was on the point of summoning Betty to show him out when the maid poked her head about the door. The housemaid was holding the handle close to her body with just her face and mobcap visible at an angle.

'What is it, Betty?' Helen asked quickly, alarmed by her servant's odd appearance.

Betty took a nimble sideways step over the threshold and tried to immediately shut the door behind her. It was to no avail. She was suddenly sent flying as the door was shoved fully open and a stout gentleman barged in to the parlour. He was garbed in a brown wool coat and beneath a burly arm was squashed his hat.

'Is this him?' Samuel Drover loudly demanded, forgoing introduction or explanation for his outrageous intrusion. His balding pate was snapped down in the direction of Jason. 'Is it him?' he again insisted on knowing. His scalp remained low and pointing straight ahead, although his eyes had swivelled to bulge at Helen.

Helen blinked rapidly, momentarily shocked to speech-lessness.

'I told him you was prior engaged with company, ma'am,' Betty mumbled, miserably aware of her mistress's petrified consternation. 'He don't never listen. He just pushed past…uncouth he is…'

Samuel Drover was unaffected by that slur on his character. 'Is this the poor fellow?' he purred sarcastically. He eyed the imposing gentleman stationed by the mantelpiece, a dark hand braced on pale marble and a faintly bemused expression shaping his beautifully stern features. 'I must say he don't look to be on his uppers.' Mr. Drover subjected Jason to a calculating inspection. 'I reckon this person could find fifty-three pounds two shillings and five halfpenny in his pocket right now.' With that he whipped a bill from somewhere inside his coat and begun to stride purposefully forward.

Having finally shaken herself from her daze, Helen said in a quaver, 'Mr Drover, please wait in the hallway and I will—' She broke off to skip over the oak boards as Samuel Drover continued his menacing advance towards Jason.

Helen deftly interposed her petite figure between the belligerent grocer and the muscular physique of her new landlord. She stood with her chin elevated and her back to Jason as though she would protect him from assault…or having his pockets picked. With her countenance alternating between shocked pallor and pink mortification, she announced, 'Mr Drover! Listen to me! This gentleman is most definitely *not* my brother, I cannot impress on you strongly enough that I resent…' Helen's impassioned plea was curtailed as firm hands, gentle as a caress, enclosed her upper arms. Suddenly she was lifted a little way off the ground and then deposited carefully at Jason's side.

Mr Drover tottered back a step as a broad hand suddenly shot towards him.

'I don't think we have been properly introduced. I am Sir Jason Hunter.'

Samuel Drover glared suspiciously at the five elegant digits extended towards him.

Having clapped his eyes on a gentleman with dark hair and a handsome visage, at his ease inside Westlea House, Samuel was impressed enough by the likeness between the couple to have decided this must be the tight-fist to whom Mrs Marlowe was related. 'How can I be sure you're not this lady's brother?' he queried whilst giving a single pump to Jason's hand.

'Should you demand proof, my mother, I think, would attest to my legitimacy, having first planted you a facer.' It was no empty jest. The Dowager Lady Hunter was renowned for a fiery temperament that remained unabated despite her having recently reached the stately decade of a sexagenarian.

Samuel Drover's eyes squinted upwards in consideration. Defeated, he muttered, 'Well, whoever you say you are, I want my cash. And don't try to pull a fast one and take your custom elsewhere. I'll tell every other merchant hereabouts to avoid your business. Don't think I won't.'

Numb with humiliation Helen could only watch glassily as Jason suddenly took Mr Drover's shoulder in what looked to be an exceedingly firm grip. Five fingers bit further into brown wool as the man tried to shrug him off.

'I think you have made your point,' Jason said.

'If you're not Kingston, where is he? Do you know?' The grocer gave Helen a hard stare. 'Mrs Marlowe thinks to keep that information from me. I'll find out his direction and set the duns on him.'

'I understand your predicament, sir,' Jason said equably, steering Samuel about with one hand in quite a facile fashion. 'However, as you can see, Mrs Marlowe's brother is not here, so you appear to be wasting your time and your threats.'

'I'll take back the sack of potatoes, or what's left of it, that my boy brought here last week.' Mr Drover aimed that over his shoulder at Helen as Jason propelled him towards the door.

'I'll bid you good afternoon, Mrs Marlowe,' Jason said as he paused for a moment on the threshold. His easy stance seemed in no way affected by the restriction he was imposing on the fidgeting merchant.

Helen fleetingly met his gaze and a flicker of gentleness in his eyes put a peculiar sensation in the pit of her stomach. *Don't pity me!* It was a silent, heartfelt demand that threatened to burst the sob swelling in her chest. Quickly she lowered her prickling eyes to her tightly laced fingers. Unaware that Jason had nudged the florid-faced grocer forward into the hallway, she managed an imperceptible nod at an empty doorway. 'Yes…good day to you, sir….'

* * *

'You look as though you've lost a sovereign and found a shilling.'

Jason scowled at his brother as he passed him. By the time Mark Hunter had turned on the sweeping staircase, peered at his brother's flying heels, then hared after him, Jason had strode the length of a thickly carpeted corridor. He slammed into his study, downed two shots of whisky one after the other and was refilling his glass when Mark appeared.

'Bad time at the tables?' Mark's tone was sympathetic as he speculated on a possible, if unlikely, cause of his brother's dark disposition. He helped himself to Jason's decanter and, after a couple of gulps from his glass, realised his commiserations remained unappreciated. He tried a blunter approach. 'Devil take it, Jay, if you've not lost at cards, what's up with you now? It's too much, I tell you, having to continually look at your long face. You've been odd for weeks.'

Jason let his lean frame drop into the chair positioned behind a grand oak desk. Having settled himself with his boots resting on the table edge, he slanted his brother a stare over the rim of his glass. 'When did my moods become your damned business? And why is it every time I come home, you're here? I don't remember inviting you to move in.' His brother's pained expression caused him to blow out his cheeks and gesture apology with a flick of a hand.

'I know the old goat wants shooting for acting so blasted idiotic,' Mark intoned with some indignation. 'But, even if the two women are good friends, it don't just affect *your* mistress, y'know. Every bachelor in town is cursing over it, so no need to take it out on me if Diana is being tricky.'

Jason grunted a laugh at his brother's oblique and garbled reference to a rumour that he'd personally found amusing rather than irritating.

He had heard the talk that his paramour was jealous of her friend Mrs Bertram. That woman had, if gossip was to be believed, secured a promise from Lord Frobisher that he would make an honest woman of her before the year was out, thus making her a lady in name, if not in nature.

Jason carefully placed down his empty glass, feeling a little the worse for alcohol. On the way home he had called in at White's and loitered, drinking, for an hour or more, hoping that George Kingston might turn up, simply so he could knock down the mean bastard.

'It's nothing to do with Diana or any foolish aspirations she might have,' he told his brother.

'Relieved to hear it,' Mark replied with a grin. 'So what has upset—?'

'Mark…go away.' Jason advised with guttural gentility.

Mark noticed a flare of threat in his brother's eyes and shrugged. He knew from past experience when it was wise to retreat and leave Jason alone to brood. He strolled to the door, whistling.

Jason rested his dark head against the hide chair-back and stared sightlessly at the ceiling. His features were tensely set, but a muscle moving close to his mouth animated his mask-like visage.

His brother's instinct that a woman was stoking his frustration was quite correct, even if he was ignorant of her identity.

Helen Marlow had unexpectedly come back into his life and he couldn't chase from his mind the exquisite woman who had emerged from the bonny child he'd known. He wished now that he'd sought to renew their acquaintance sooner. He could have done so, for he'd spied her at a distance on odd occasions. It would have been simple enough to approach her and ask how she fared. But the feud with George had driven a wedge between them years ago when she was still a schoolgirl. Later, when she returned to town as a young widow to live with her father, it seemed too much time had passed and they had slipped back to being virtual strangers.

It had been more than ten years since he had come within touching distance of her. From the moment she had opened the door of Westlea House to him and tried to hide her dishevelled appearance behind the wood panels, he had been robbed of his peace of mind. In truth, he resented the loss.

Yet his thoughts continually revolved around finding excuses to go back and see her again. The urge to do so was not primarily altruistic and therein lay the root of his torment. He wanted to improve her lot in life, but he desired her, too, and she knew it.

He gave a lopsided smile at the ceiling as he recalled the way she had instinctively leaped to defend him when the grocer got belligerent. Feelings of tenderness had engulfed Jason as she'd stood before him like an intrepid waif prepared to do battle. He'd also felt a sense of relief, for she had proven—unintentionally, he imagined—that she was not completely set against him. She was indebted to him through no fault of her own and she sensed that made her vulnerable to his lust. In just a short while she had displayed wit and courage and dignity. She had also showed her selfish brother more loyalty than George would merit in his lifetime. But acknowledging Helen had fine qualities had not subdued the throb in his loins.

He had a perfectly adequate mistress. Why would he want the trouble of wooing into bed a well-bred woman who thought him a rake and seemed unwilling to trust him to act ethically? Something else was nettling him. Jason knew he was playing too easily into George Kingston's hands. He was allowing George to manipulate him, yet seemed unable to put a stop to it. George wanted him to take over the financial burden of his sisters' keep and he was achieving his aim with such ease that he had begun to dispense with the need to be subtle. Filling the empty grates and larders at Westlea House was not his responsibility. But he had taken on the task, just as George intended he should. George had gambled on a meeting between Helen and him paying spectacular dividends, and he had won. George was now basking in his victory. He was goading him, blatantly challenging him to choose between pride and lust.

Jason knew that soon he would have to make a decision before gossip started. Evicting Helen and her sister from Westlea House was out of the question, but it would not be long before it was common knowledge he owned the property.

Risking a stain on Charlotte's reputation was also out of the question. The obvious solution would be to establish a position in his life for Helen.

Wife or mistress? George Kingston would not care either way. If Mrs Marlowe became a kept woman, polite society would be provided with a tasty morsel of gossip for a week or two, but they would not ostracise her. Helen's reputation was protected by the status conferred by her late husband.

Thus, it was his choice which role he offered to her after such a limited renewal of their acquaintance. Certainly she fascinated him and he was sure he liked her, but he had felt that way before about young women who now he could barely recall to mind.

Jason got to his feet, only half-aware that he had come to a decision as he stretched out his stiff muscles. A rueful smile tugged at a corner of his mouth as he realised that the only objections he was likely to receive to an offer of *carte blanche* was from the lady herself.

Chapter Eight

'What on earth is the matter?'

Helen had been attempting to compose a letter of apology to Jason Hunter while Charlotte was out. The scuffed leather surface on the bureau was littered with crumpled scraps of paper, testament to the difficulty of the task she'd set herself.

But now Charlotte was back and looking very dejected. Pushing away pen and paper, Helen swivelled on her seat. Charlotte was plucking at her hat strings with vibrating fingers. Once free of her thick tresses, the bonnet was forcefully discarded on to the sofa. Charlotte sank down beside it, her red-rimmed eyes concealed by her palms.

'What is it, dear?' Helen immediately went to her. She crouched by the side of the chair with an anxious frown crinkling her ivory brow. Charlotte's hands were gently eased from her face and Helen comforted them with her own. 'What has happened? Is Philip not with you?' Helen glanced at the door. Philip invariably came in for a short while when he brought Charlotte home from an outing. 'Have you argued?' It was a doubtfully tendered possibility. Charlotte and Philip usually seemed a very harmonious couple.

Charlotte raised her watery brown eyes to Helen's face. 'Philip won't ever come here again. He won't marry me now. Why would he when I have such a hateful brother?' she gritted out through small pearly teeth. Charlotte again hid her freshly streaming eyes with her fingers.

Helen sank forward on to her knees as an inkling of what might be ailing her sister put a guilty sigh in her throat. So obsessed had she been with dwelling on her fraught encounter with Jason Hunter and Mr Drover that she had neglected to give any more thought to a worrying incident that had occurred before either of those gentleman had arrived.

Helen cast back her mind a few hours. Charlotte had been from the room, collecting her coat, when George had cruelly curtailed Philip's attempt to make formal his suit. No doubt Philip had felt injured enough by George's churlish rejection to tell Charlotte of it.

Helen remembered, too, with heavy heart, that George had not been content to leave it at that. Once their sister had quit the house with the Goodes, George had more doom to deliver on the subject of the courting couple. Or rather, he had anticipated that she would do his dirty work for him. His curt dictate echoed in her mind: *I do not want Charlotte seeing him any more. Make that clear to her or I will make it clear to him. And, as you have just noticed, I shall not stand on ceremony when I do so.*

'Was Philip annoyed that George was short with him? He had every right to be…'

'What did he say to Philip?' Charlotte interrupted, scrubbing the heel of a hand across her eyes. 'Tell me, please! I sensed something unpleasant had occurred while I was getting ready to go out. Philip is too agreeable to make a fuss, but I guessed something was wrong, even before George came over and was horrible to us in the park.'

'You saw George whilst you were out?'

Charlotte nodded. 'I'm sure George only turned up in Hyde Park because he guessed we had gone there. Why does he hate Philip? He has never taken the trouble to get to know him.'

Helen tightened her grip on Charlotte's shivery hands. 'I'm sure he does not hate him,' she soothed. 'It is just that our brother is…' She struggled to find words that might mitigate George's boorishness. 'I know our brother has an unfortunate manner at times,' she lamely concluded.

'*Unfortunate manner?*' Charlotte shrieked and stamped a foot to emphasise her outrage. 'He is a swine! He deliberately humiliated Philip in front of his sister and me! The park was quite crowded too and a lot of people witnessed what went on. A horrible fellow started laughing at us.' Charlotte's voice wobbled as she recounted, 'Poor Anne was so upset she started to cry, although she pretended she just had a speck in her eye.'

Helen's wide eyes revealed her astonishment at what she'd heard. Usually George sought to keep his shameful behaviour out of public display. 'What exactly did he do?' she demanded to know.

'We had stopped by the lake to watch the swans and George just appeared with one of his cronies. George got out of his carriage and stormed over to us. With no more ado he ordered me home. Philip was startled by his rudeness, but took it in good part, I thought. I'm sure he knew George was slighting him because he doesn't deem him good enough for me.' She paused to wipe a hand across her feverishly flushed cheeks. 'Philip offered to immediately bring me back, but George stared at him as though he was dirt beneath his shoe. He snapped out that he would directly take me *safely* home himself.' Charlotte pulled a scrap of linen from a pocket. She furiously applied it to her glistening dark eyes. 'Philip was…he looked so mortified when George made me get out of the gig. That's when I heard his friend laughing.' She gurgled a sob, then wiped her dewy nose. 'I tried to reassure Philip that I was disgusted too by George's behaviour. I said I would be pleased to see him again later in the week. But he avoided my eye and said, in a strange voice, that he didn't think that would be possible.' Charlotte blinked away fresh tears. 'He doesn't want to see me again. It is finished between us, I know it is.'

Helen shot to her feet. 'George brought you home? Where is he?' she demanded and flew to the window to peer out into the street.

'He is gone. The whole way home he wouldn't speak to me, even when I shouted at him that he was overbearing. When we turned into the Square he cast on me one of his black looks.' Charlotte pursed her lips mutinously. 'He said he would never give his consent to a man of Goode's standing and I might as well get used to it. That's when I told him he was the vilest man alive and I would marry whomever I chose and *he* might as well get used to it. After that it was as much as he could do to help me down from the carriage. He was so rough with me I feared he might pull my arm from its socket. Before Betty had let me in he'd set off up the street.'

Helen observed Charlotte's distress and her heart went out to her. It was difficult to comprehend why any decent person would deliberately make a spectacle of a gentleman as inoffensive as Philip Goode. But then George, she reluctantly admitted to herself, had not acted very decently in a long while. Despite knowing it, she still felt lurking within her a sibling's sadness. A corrosive resentment of the contented, and a grasping wife, were destroying the personable brother who once had taught her how to ride her first pony and fish the streams in the Surrey countryside.

Helen retraced her steps to the sofa and sat down close to Charlotte. 'From what you have said it seems George has made himself, rather than Philip, appear ridiculous. It is George who needs our pity,' she added gravely. 'Perhaps if he had made a successful marriage he might not be so sour at life.' She enclosed her sister in a hug and planted a kiss on her luxuriant, auburn tangles. 'We are the lucky ones, Charlotte. You and I both have known what bliss there is in being cherished by someone we love. Poor George! I think at times he knows what he misses and is bitterly jealous.'

Charlotte rested her head on Helen's slender shoulder. 'I wish Papa was here. He would have liked Philip. He would have given us his blessing…just as he did to you and Harry.'

'Yes, he would. Philip is very like Harry. I expect that is why I took to him from the start.' With a wistful smile she looked down at her young sister. 'But our papa is not here. Neither is dearest Harry.' She put Charlotte from her and said briskly, 'So we must look after ourselves and not let our brother scare the fight out of us.'

'I do love Philip, you know.'

'Yes, I do know. And that is why, somehow or other, you must marry him,' Helen answered softly. She looked off into the distance with a slight frown drawing close her ebony brows. 'I expect Philip wants very much to see you again, but fears sparking another ugly scene with George. And who could blame him for that?' She gave Charlotte an encouraging smile. 'The best thing will be for me to go alone and pay the Goodes a visit. I shall let them know that they are most welcome to call on us at any time. If George gets temperamental over it…well, he shall have me to contend with.'

'Beg pardon, Mrs Marlowe, but he is back again.'

Helen peered over her sister's tousled head at Betty. Her maidservant was, once more that day, stationed in the doorway with an apologetic look on her face. Helen sensed her heart falter and then a burst of terrified exhilaration made her feel quite light-headed. In a breathy rush she demanded, 'Who is it, Betty?'

'Oh, not the gentleman, ma'am,' Betty said with distinct disappointment. 'It's Mr Drover. He won't say what he wants, so I've left him on the step this time.'

Within a moment Helen was briskly walking to the front door. 'My brother is still not here, Mr Drover,' she announced without preamble. 'And I am not expecting him to arrive any time soon. I'm very sorry, but I cannot help you.'

'I've not come about him.' The grocer shifted on the stone step, fingering the brim of the hat that he was banging in rhythm against his knees. 'I'm sorry for acting hot-headed earlier…end of tether, you understand.' He cleared his throat. 'The other gentleman settled my account.' His tone was level, but a sly glance slanted up at her before he again meekly studied his shoes. 'I've fetched over that order you sent with my boy earlier in the week.'

'Sir Jason Hunter has settled the bill…' Helen whispered. It was not really a question at all. Since Jason had been rudely petitioned to pay for her groceries, she had wondered if he might indeed do so.

Helen suddenly became conscious that Betty was hovering behind her. The young woman's gaping mouth and bulging eyes indicated her great interest in the proceedings. Before Helen could dismiss her entranced maid, Samuel Drover supplied both women with another piece of riveting information.

'The gentleman left cash on your account, too, so you're not to fret on this load.' He gave a sideways nod at his cart. After a silent few seconds he politely queried, 'Shall I start to bring it in?'

'Please do.' It was a firm instruction from Helen, issued after only a tiny hesitation.

Mr Drover lowered his head and humbly backed away a step or two before setting about his task.

Helen proudly elevated her chin. 'Please set fires in the parlour and the bedchambers. Then when the provisions are checked we will plan what to prepare for dinner.'

'Yes, ma'am,' Betty agreed in a buoyant tone.

Charlotte's bright words, issued from the parlour's doorway, reassured Helen that her sister had observed, if not heard, what went on. 'Heavens! Do you think that George is feeling so guilty over his foul behaviour this afternoon that he has paid the bill at last and sent us some food?'

Helen subdued the sour laugh that scratched at her throat and limited her response to a wry smile. She did not intend to lie to her sister over the source of their improved fortune. But omitting to mention who was their benefactor might be wise until she had a notion of how to present it all to Charlotte.

Besides, Charlotte now seemed too embroiled in her own tribulations to bother with mundane domesticity even if a tasty meal and a warm bedchamber were finally in the offing. Helen could tell that her sister was again lost in her own thoughts as she fiddled with her hat ribbons and sighed loudly. 'Why do you not go and freshen yourself, Charlotte? Put a brush through your hair and wash your teary cheeks before we dine.'

Charlotte sucked in a rejuvenating breath. With a little nod she turned towards the stairs. Halfway up the flight she pivoted towards Helen with a plea that proved her thoughts were indeed fixed on her beloved. 'Will you promise me that very soon you will go and see Philip? Please tell him that I am so sorry and that—'

'Hush!' Helen interrupted Charlotte, but she gave her an indulgent smile. 'I have said I will go there and so I shall.'

In a moment Charlotte had skipped out of sight and Betty had bustled into view with the coal scuttle.

Helen quite expected to hear the sounds of Mr Drover whistling and Betty humming a tune. She felt heat flood her complexion as she imagined what occupied their minds as they happily went about their business. The grocer and her servant had come to the same conclusion about what prompted *the gentleman's* intervention in her domestic affairs. It had improved their attitudes enormously to think that she was paying in kind for her keep. Helen didn't for one moment blame either of them for suspecting such an arrangement existed. Had she not already challenged Jason Hunter to clarify what motivated his benevolence? She had received no proper answer from him and was still unsure what prompted him to be generous. But the thought of accepting his charity or his pity was anathema to her.

She could, of course, leave the food on the cart and the coal in the bunker. Charlotte and she could swallow their pride and scrape an existence on Rowan Walk instead of in Westlea House.

Helen felt tranquillity trickle through her as an inner battle ebbed. In her mind it was settled, and there was nothing new or daring about her plan. A host of women before her had resorted to a discreet liaison to keep themselves and their families clothed and fed. He seemed honest and generous and there was nothing about his person that revolted her…quite the reverse… As to her part, she was sure that she could adopt a brazen attitude and willingness. She glanced at her dowdy appearance and gave a wry smile. Perhaps a little artifice with a needle and a rouge pot might not go amiss either.

A little breath caught in her throat as she contemplated the decision she'd made. She might try to be rational and practical, but there was no denying Sir Jason was a powerful and exciting man. What if her proposition was rebuffed, or worse, mocked? Helen felt a fluttering in her abdomen as she imagined dealing with the humiliation of his rejection. The feeling strengthened as she imagined dealing with his agreement to her suggestion! She felt heat seep into her complexion at the haunting memory of making love with Harry. Would she want to again have the sensation of a man's hot skin welded to hers when, perhaps, he might not even like her very much? She quickly concentrated on Jason's kindness to her, the intensity of his grey gaze when he looked at her. He liked her at the very least, she was sure of it!

'It looks as though Bridgeman has forgiven George for not selling him Westlea House.'

Mark Hunter's cynical observation drew his brother's interest. Jason dropped the opera glasses from his eyes and turned to look to his left.

Colin Bridgeman and George Kingston were indeed looking very cosy together in one of the boxes. Bridgeman had
his head tipped back and was guffawing. Of Iris Kingston
there was no sign, although Jason had seen George and his
wife arrive together. Jason's coach had drawn up outside the
opera house at the same time as had George's. The gentlemen
had coolly acknowledged one another with a nod. The ladies
had exchanged disdainful summarising stares. Diana's audi-
ble aside that a far superior harlot would be needed to put *her*
in her place had made Jason inwardly smile as they proceeded
to the stairs in the King's Theatre.

The house had been scintillating with light and laughter as
Jason and Diana took their seats in one of the green boxes just
before the performance started.

Now the curtain had fallen on the first act and a buzz of conversation was again growing louder in the auditorium. The
performance had been pleasing, but now the main entertainment had begun as people flitted from place to place to pose
with friends and gossip over the latest *on dits*. Mark Hunter
had moments ago ambled in to speak to his brother, leaving
behind in his own box his current amour. The abandoned ac-
tress was with her gallants, yet her soulful eyes were constantly straying to Mark despite the fact that he appeared
oblivious to her attention.

Soon after Mark had arrived in Jason's box, Diana had left
it. Jason had made no objection when one of his mistress's
young admirers had entered his domain. The fresh-faced

boy had politely asked if he might escort Mrs Tucker to Lord Frobisher's box where her friend Mrs Bertram was holding court.

The appearance of the eager young buck hovering behind him had started Jason reminiscing on his own youth. For the past few minutes he had been idly training his glasses on the pit to watch the boisterous gentlemen congregating there. Fifteen or more years ago it would have been he and his friends—George Kingston included—laughing and joking whilst fixing a lascivious eye on the elegant females up in the boxes. It had been a game amongst young bloods then, as he imagined it was now, to compete for a lady's signal. Wagers had regularly been laid on who would be first to be beckoned by a society beauty to indulge in a little flirtation…perhaps more than that before the night was out.

Jason had been following, with some lazy interest, the interaction between Michael Langham and Lady Corbin. The ageing countess had finally given up on subtlety. Her bosom was spilling from her gown as she hung over the edge of her box, frantically jiggling her fan at the object of her desire.

But now Jason lounged back in his chair, bored with the mating rituals of the beau monde. His eyes narrowed on the two gentlemen to one side of him, still deep in conversation.

'I'd not be surprised if George were negotiating some sort of deal with Bridgeman,' Mark suggested with a quirk of a dark eyebrow. 'Can't be selling him his wife, though.' He gave a coarse chuckle. 'I hear Bridgeman's had Iris for free.'

'As have above half the gentlemen here tonight,' Jason murmured on extending his muscular legs comfortably in front of him.

'I saw those two together in Hyde Park yesterday. Kingston made quite a spectacle of his youngest sister, and the people she was with, much to Bridgeman's amusement.'

Jason slowly drew himself up in his chair again and rested his elbows on his knees. He turned his face to Mark and gave him his full attention. 'What happened?' he asked.

Mark shrugged. 'At a guess I'd say George was casting aspersions on the worth of the young gentleman taking his sister for a drive. I don't know why, he seemed mannerly, and there was another lady present so the niceties seemed to be in order.' He frowned thoughtfully. 'I was ready to intervene when I eventually recognised the poor fellow's identity, but it would have simply prolonged the hubbub. We may not be close, but there is a family connection. Goode looked ready to explode with embarrassment and his sister, Anne seemed to be crying. Kingston can be damned insensitive.'

Jason stared at his linked fingers, then slanted a steady gaze at his brother. 'Philip Goode was taking Charlotte Kingston for a drive?'

Mark gave a nod. 'For the last time, I'd say, judging by Kingston's reaction. If the lad had ideas above his station where George's sister was concerned, I'd say he's been knocked severely back into place.'

'Which means that Kingston must have another candidate in mind or he wouldn't stir himself to bother,' Jason muttered. He took a thoughtful look at George Kingston's box.

Mark read his brother's mind. 'I've heard that Bridgeman is in the market for a wife.'

At that point Diana swept into Jason's box in a haze of cream muslin and gardenias. She pouted her thanks at her ardent gallant for safely returning her whilst keeping an eye on Jason to detect a reaction. The fact that there was none, and Jason continued conversing in a low voice with his brother, made spots of colour burn in her cheeks. She settled herself in her chair with much rustling and sighing.

The curtain began to open on the second act and Mark took his leave to return to his own seat.

Jason looked at Diana; she rewarded his indolent attention with an extremely seductive smile.

'Mrs Bertram and I were just saying that the soprano sounds shrill tonight.'

'Do you want to go?' Jason suggested bluntly.

Diana's lashes lowered to screen a sudden brightness in her blue eyes. 'I'm not bothered if we do leave. I know you'll always find us something pleasing to do. Are you bored? Have you something nice in mind?' She whispered huskily.

Jason straightened his spine against the chair-back, then lithely gained his feet. Courteously he extended a hand to Diana. 'Nothing in particular,' he said lazily, his eyes on the dim outline of George Kingston's box. 'But I've seen enough….'

Chapter Nine

It had been some months since Helen had set foot in this house, but she saw straight away that the broken hallway chair was still propped against the wall. An air of faded elegance imbued the vestibule of the Goodes' residence much as it did the interior of Westlea House. Walters, the family's old retainer, closed the front door behind Helen before turning to give her a stump-toothed smile.

'Miss Anne will be pleased to see you, Mrs Marlowe.'

'I…actually, is Mr Philip Goode at home?' Helen asked. 'It would be nice to see him too whilst I am here.'

'He is at home, Mrs Marlowe but he has an important gentleman with him at present.' The information was imparted with a hint of confidentiality and a twinkle in the eye. Walters was plainly impressed by the fellow's identity if not about to reveal it.

'Helen! It is good to see you. Is Charlotte not with you?'

Helen twisted about to see Anne Goode flitting down the stairs. 'Charlotte is indisposed…a slight headache, but nothing to worry about,' Helen quickly added as Anne showed concern. 'Perhaps I ought come back another time as you have company.'

'No, please stay!' Anne urged. 'Come to the drawing room. Philip will like to see you.' She linked arms with Helen. 'I had just slipped away from there for a second to change into my best shawl when I thought I recognised your voice.' Anne gave an absent stroke to the lustrous silk swathing arms that were lightly freckled. 'I think our distinguished visitor is only planning to stay a short time. Do come and say hello for it might delay him. I'll wager he is too mannerly to take his leave soon after someone new is introduced.' Anne gave a little giggle. 'It is hard to credit that we are related to such a grand family. In fact, it is so long since Goodes socialised with Hunters that I had quite forgot our connection.'

'Hunters?' Helen's tone held sharp enquiry.

Helen abruptly halted and Anne was jerked about to face her, for their arms were still entwined as they took a promenade along the hallway. Being so close Anne spontaneously hugged Helen in excitement.

'Sir Jason Hunter is visiting us. We are distant cousins, you know,' she proudly informed her.

A startled tenseness shaped Helen's features on discovering the identity of the eminent guest.

'Do you know the Hunters?' Anne asked on a frown.

Helen managed to execute a jerky nod. 'Sir Jason and my brother, George, were friends when younger. When we lived in Surrey our house was quite close to Thorne Park.' The explanation was brief and abstracted—already Helen's mind was attending to the consequences of what she'd heard.

She had promised Charlotte that she would relay a message to Philip today, but she needed an opportunity to be alone with him. With Jason Hunter present there would be even less chance to engineer a private conversation and discover if her sister was to have her heart broken.

But there were other issues besides Charlotte's happiness rotating dizzily in her mind. When she had left Westlea House this afternoon her first task had been to take to the post a letter for Jason Hunter. In it she conveyed her regrets at Mr Drover's conduct, but its proper purpose was to ask him to again visit her. She was reasonably confident that her phrasing and his sophistication would ensure he understood her objective.

Infuriatingly, the two gentlemen with whom she had pressing business were in the immediate vicinity, yet nothing would be gained by seeing either of them now.

It seemed an odd coincidence that Jason Hunter should have recently renewed his acquaintance with her and also with distant cousins he had not seen in an age. Helen felt inclined to ponder if it was connected to the association between Charlotte and Philip.

Charlotte had defiantly told their brother that she would marry Philip despite his objections. George did not like to be thwarted and could bear ferocious grudges. The roses, put in Helen's cheeks by her brisk walk, faded away. Her reasoning veered between possibility and probability. Had George stooped to enrol Jason's help in ensuring Philip stayed away? There was no love lost between her brother and Jason Hunter, but she had bitter proof that they could successfully deal together in business.

'Are you well, Helen? You look very pale,' Anne said anxiously.

Helen reassured her friend with a smile.

'Will you come to the drawing room and join us? You need not feel overawed by Sir Jason,' Anne advised helpfully. 'Indeed, he is terrifyingly distinguished and handsome.' A little shiver of delight accompanied that observation. 'But he is not at all uppity.' Anne inclined her head to whisper, 'I think I have a crush on him already and he has not been here above half an hour. I know his brother Mark is handsome, too. I've heard that Emily Beaumont has quite a hankering for him.' She sighed. 'It is a shame that Mama is gone out. She will be distraught to have missed him.'

Gently Helen disengaged her arm from her friend's. 'I shall not stay, Anne.' The idea that she might manage to politely converse with Jason in company, knowing that her explicit summons was even now on its way to his door, was enough to make her complexion flood with blood.

Anne skimmed the back of her hand over Helen's cheek. 'Heavens! First you seemed too pale now you look very flushed. I hope that you and Charlotte have not taken a chill.'

'I shall be on my way, Anne. I only called in as I was passing this way to go to the library.' It was a little fib that she could make truth by entering that establishment on her way home. 'Charlotte is on her own, so it would perhaps be best that I do not tarry.'

Once back in mellow sunshine Helen descended the stone steps and turned in the direction of home. As she passed the phaeton at the kerb she hesitated. Belatedly she recognised it and chided herself for having overlooked it when she arrived. Twice recently this very vehicle had been idle outside Westlea House. She glanced at the young groom holding the reins of the fine chestnut horses as she walked swiftly on.

Jason accepted more tea from Walters and wandered to the window with it. He glanced down at the street scene, half-aware that Anne had returned and was bestowing on him another coquettish smile. His mouth tilted in response as his cup travelled upwards. Short of its target the vessel hovered, then was replaced softly on its saucer. He turned fully to gaze through the glass at the girlish figure skipping quickly down the stone steps. The young woman lingered by his phaeton, long enough for him to clearly identify her, before hurrying away.

In Anne's absence he'd had an enlightening conversation with her brother. By calling on them today he'd finally broken the ice that had been set half a century ago by their warring kin. He'd remained an acceptable amount of time. Now he was ready to take his leave.

Helen had been walking quickly, her face lowered against gusts that whipped her hair into her eyes. She had slowed her pace to pick away the irritating tendrils and clear her vision. Now, as she raised her head, she glimpsed him just in time to compose herself.

The phaeton had drawn to the kerb a little way in front of her and Jason was leaning against the shiny coachwork, watching her approach.

Helen felt her stomach somersault at the sight of him. There was no doubt that Anne was correct: Jason Hunter, despite his casual stance and his dark fringe blown awry by the breeze, was terrifyingly attractive.

She remembered that she had planned on looking sophisticatedly groomed the next time they met. She knew the rudiments of applying cosmetics and could make an adequate job of tinting her lips and complexion. She had also been rather pleased with the way her thick tresses had been teased into a stylish coiffure when she had practised with the tongs earlier in the week.

With a wry inner smile Helen acknowledged that today she looked simply bedraggled, whereas he looked ruggedly windswept. But her steps didn't falter as she brushed the black tangles from her white skin and neared him.

He was watching her, a slant to his mouth, and she knew he was amused to see how she would react to this unexpected meeting; whether she would stop and talk or simply nod and walk on by. But then he had not yet received her schematic note and had no idea that, in fact, a meeting between them was exactly what she wanted. It was merely the time and place that were wrong.

Her chin tilted and she boldly traversed the pavement to stand before him. 'Good day to you, Sir Jason. How are you?'

Jason inclined his head. 'I'm very well, thank you. And how are you, Mrs Marlowe?'

'I'm well, too, sir, thank you.'

'And the weather seems quite fine for this time of the year,' he added smoothly. Slate-grey eyes skimmed the perfect oval of her face as she attempted to gather the loose strands clinging to her complexion. 'Though it is perhaps a little too windy.' It was a murmured observation.

Helen felt her face burn where his darkly humorous gaze lingered.

'Why did you not stay longer at the Goodes?'

'Anne mentioned to you that I had called?'

'No. I saw you leaving from the drawing-room window.'

'Oh…' Helen caught her lower lip in small perfect teeth. She settled on being honest. 'I…I wanted to speak privately to Philip about something, but it didn't seem that I had chosen an appropriate time.'

'I thought perhaps Anne mentioned my name and you sped away to avoid seeing me.'

'Yes, she did. But, no, I didn't…run away, that is. Actually, I have wanted to see you and have today sent you a letter.' Helen abruptly pressed her lips together. She had not meant to so boldly disclose that fact. But he had guessed correctly her evasive action, and it had nettled her into rashness. She strove to limit the damage. 'I…I wrote to you because there is something on my mind…but please don't ask me to explain now,' she quickly besought as his eyes became narrow with interest.

'Perhaps I can guess what it is,' he softly said. 'You want to know what ulterior motive prompted me to settle your grocery bill. Is that it?'

He was not quite correct, but his thoughts were certainly travelling in the right direction. She backed away a step, said in a strangled tone, 'It is not a good time or place to talk, sir.' She glanced about, noticing that people passing by were sliding inquisitive looks at them. No doubt they were wondering why an elegant gentleman, in possession of an expensive equipage, would be in tense conversation at the side of the road with an unstylish young woman. As Helen noticed two plump matrons give her a scandalised stare, then put their heads together, a shocked breath filled her lungs. Surely nobody thought her to be soliciting! The thought that next jolted into her mind crushed her indignation and her pride. Procuring this man's protection was exactly her intention; she had simply hoped to proposition him out of sight of prying eyes.

Jason's head tilted so he might study her lowered face. 'If you have taken the trouble to write to me about your concerns, they are obviously important.' He held out an arm to her. 'Come, if you will allow me take you home, we can talk there—'

'No…' Helen swiftly interrupted, her eyes glancing on his. 'Charlotte is at home today and I would rather not…'

'I understand. I'm sure I can find a place en route to Westlea House that is neither too secluded nor too public. A drive through the park is sure to turn up a quiet spot. We can stop there and look at the view without attracting attention.'

Helen needed little persuasion to agree. As soon as he returned home he would have her note…and her measure. It would be best to surge ahead with what she'd started. If she had misjudged his interest in her, and her forwardness irritated rather than pleased him, she might never see him again. She knew that he found Diana Tucker desirable and, Heaven only knew, she was as far removed in face and figure from her as a woman could be. As Helen took his arm to be courteously assisted aboard his phaeton, she drove down any regrets at having despatched the letter at all. The deed was done, and done after much inner debate that had kept her restless throughout last night.

She had been expecting that, once on the move, he would immediately try to prise some snippet from her. But she was wrong. It was several minutes later that Helen abruptly broke the silence. She had become far too conscious of a muscular thigh encased in fawn fabric close to her hip. Feeling flustered by his proximity, she slid a few inches away on the seat before angling to face him. Briskly she marshalled her courage and her thoughts. She might just as well open proceedings and contrive to lead their conversation towards revealing herself…as a brazen hussy. Quickly she blurted, 'I know that you are related to the Goodes, sir; forgive me for asking, but what prompted you to visit them after so long an estrangement?'

Without losing speed, Jason skilfully manoeuvred a path between two weighty coaches. Once the road was clear he reined back the plunging horses and gave her a glance. 'Are you asking whether the friendship between your sister and Philip Goode might have spurred me to go there?'

There was very little hesitation from Helen before she owned up to that. 'Yes, sir, I suppose I am.'

Jason smiled his appreciation that she'd not prevaricated. 'I suppose I could say I simply thought a family feud of some decades' duration had run its course, and it was time to extend an olive branch.'

'But?'

'But it wouldn't be the whole truth.'

Emboldened by his honesty, Helen continued to probe. 'Did you know that Philip has been quietly courting my sister, Charlotte?'

'I had heard something of the sort.'

'From George, I take it.' Her spontaneous response was curt enough to make Jason frown.

They had passed through the gates of Hyde Park. The earliness of the hour and the buffeting wind ensured that few other people were about to enjoy the spring sunshine. Jason drew the phaeton to a smooth halt in a quiet avenue. Soft afternoon sun filtered through swaying branches to lightly gild them.

'I first learned of it from my brother, Mark,' he eventually answered her.

'Your brother?' Helen echoed in surprise.

Jason turned on the seat to face her. He leaned back against the side of the vehicle. 'Mark witnessed a rather unpleasant scene in this park. It involved your brother and sister and our cousins. Mark interpreted what he saw as George displaying disapproval of Philip Goode squiring your sister.'

Helen looked at her gloved fingers, regretting having spoken snappishly before. 'That is exactly what did occur and Charlotte was mortified by the incident. She told me that George made a spectacle of them all in front of passers-by. You have confirmed our fears that gossip might ensue.'

'And are you about to confirm my fears? I get the impression you think I might have today gone, at George's behest, to tell my cousin to stay away from your sister.'

'George is determined to kill their love and find Charlotte a wealthy man. He will do whatever it takes to achieve that.'

'And you think I might help him in his ambition?'

'You do business together,' Helen said crisply, unwilling to appease the anger she sensed in him. They were being truthful with each other and she had no wish to deviate from that.

'I don't consider my cousin's courtship to be my business. But Philip and Anne Goode are kin and I take against their being made to look ridiculous. Mark was annoyed at what he saw and was tempted to intervene.'

Helen winced at the grit in his voice. 'I'm sorry if I have jumped to a wrong conclusion, sir,' she said. 'But I'm glad that your brother did not become involved. It would undoubtedly have resulted in more of a rumpus.'

'Indeed,' Jason agreed drily. 'Mark felt exactly that way.' He gazed upon her sculpted profile for a moment, fighting down an urge to reach out and feel beneath his fingertips skin that looked pale and pure as alabaster. Abruptly his gaze sought the horizon. 'Today I let Philip know I'd heard about the incident and that I deplored Kingston's conduct.'

Helen immediately swerved her golden eyes to him. She might not have had an opportunity to speak to Philip, but perhaps she could discover what Charlotte wanted to know from another source. 'Is Philip still feeling humiliated? He has every right to be angry.'

'He seemed philosophical. If you went there today to discover if he still carries a torch for your sister, the answer is that he certainly does,' Jason told her softly.

A small sweet smile from Helen displayed her gratitude at knowing it. 'Charlotte will be very happy. She was sure George had succeeded in destroying Philip's devotion.'

'If he had, perhaps it was infatuation and not worth having.'

'Oh, it's true love, I'm sure,' Helen said earnestly. 'But even so, I wouldn't blame Philip for giving it up as a lost cause. He needs George's consent to a betrothal and you've no idea how abominably rude our brother can be to him.' Helen smiled ruefully. 'A stoic temperament and an unflinching love are minimum requirements for a gentleman of limited means wishing to wed a sister of George's.'

'Was Harry Marlowe just such a man?'

'Indeed, he was, sir.' Helen felt a surge of shame that her beloved Harry be mentioned at such a time. What would Harry think of her wanton plan? A moment later she said briskly, 'Of course, my brother was then much younger and much different.' She suddenly realised that they had not yet touched on the subject of the note she had sent him.

'Are you going to tell me what is in your letter or would you rather I read it?' Jason asked as though his thoughts were in tune with hers.

Despite willing herself not to, Helen sensed a blush stain her cheeks. 'I can tell you the gist of it.' She drew in an inspiriting breath. 'First I must apologise for Mr Drover's behaviour. It was unforgivable of him—'

'But understandable. If he spoke honestly, he has been a patient man.'

Helen nodded her acceptance of that truth.

'Have you eaten well since?'

He was awaiting her reply as though her nourishment was of serious concern. 'Yes…thank you, sir, we have eaten very well. The house is warm, too.'

Jason nodded and was absently looking over parkland when he murmured, 'Good.'

'The comfort you have provided is what prompted me to write to you.' Her opening gambit was out, if uttered in an unsteady voice.

Jason picked up the leather reins from where they had rested on the seat and idly transferred them from hand to hand. 'I've explained, Mrs Marlowe, that George is due a payment from me following our recent business. Any sums I settle on your behalf will be deducted from his account. That is all there is to it. You don't owe me a damned thing.'

He was obviously irritated by this conversation to have

used strong language in front of a lady. Or…perhaps he had guessed she was about to disclose she wasn't a lady. Helen drew in a breath and blurted, 'I don't think that is absolutely true, sir.'

'What is true, then?' It was a terse demand that terminated on a laugh that sounded hollow and humourless.

Helen knew it was time to choose between acting the jade or the coquette, but unplanned words just tumbled out. 'I…I think that you have been generous to us because you have a liking for me. My reason for writing to you is…I want you to know that I have no objection to your interest. In fact, I should like to encourage it.' Her proposition ended on a soundless sob of relief that it was done.

She felt her heart thundering and inwardly she blenched—she knew her solitary attempt to win a protector had been extremely amateurish. He seemed unimpressed, too, for he remained silent, studying the leather reins crossing his palms for some while before replying.

'Perhaps if I tell you something else, Mrs Marlowe, you might reconsider some of what you've said. During our talk today I learned from Philip that he is seeking a position. I know of an opportunity in the city that might suit him. In short, if he takes up the offer, his prospects ought to improve enough for him to take a wife.'

'I am very pleased about that,' Helen said huskily, with some understatement, for her heart was soaring. 'But still I am prepared to—'

'Put yourself at my disposal?' His tone veered more to anger than irony.

'No…' Helen finally turned to look directly into his eyes. In their profound blackness she discovered a glow that calmed her. She managed a shy smile. 'No…' she repeated softly. 'I am prepared to shun modesty and propriety. Virtue has its merits, but not for someone like me; I shall not regret its loss.'

She prayed that enough was now established between them for him to take over and allow her some pride and gentility. But her hopes were dashed.

'I'm not about to make this easy for you, Helen. If it's what you want, ask me….'

Chapter Ten

'Would you make me your mistress?'

'Yes.'

'Do you not want to think about it for a moment?' Helen offered quietly.

'No. Do you?'

'No,' Helen murmured, barely faltering.

'Are you sure about that, Helen?'

'Yes…'

She had been a schoolgirl when last he had used her given name. She had always liked the way it sounded spoken in his gruff, cultured voice. Far back in her mind stirred a memory of how he would smile at her and make her feel at the same time awkward and elated and intuitive of a promise of excitement hovering between them.

But he was no longer her brother's friend, welcome in their home, and she was no longer a fanciful maid of fifteen.

She might be unpractised in such negotiations, but she knew that a gentleman was encumbered financially when he took a woman under his protection. She had anticipated that such an arrangement would necessitate a conversation between them lasting longer than a few minutes. But he seemed to have settled into staring moodily into space.

Helen was obliquely aware of his detachment whilst reasoning on what must come next flitted through her mind. Unless he intended keeping her in the background, a mistress was usually a social companion, too. Once it became common knowledge that they were lovers she would be barred from some areas of his life, but accompanying him to the theatre or a shopping trip and so on would be in her scope. Her clothes were dated and shabby. She would need an allowance for new garments in order to look acceptably stylish when partnering him. And, of course, they would need a discreet place to meet. Although he now owned the property, visiting her at Westlea House would be out of the question. Her teeth settled painfully into her lower lip as she came to shameful awareness of how naturally mercenary thoughts had occupied her. But, of course, such practicalities kept at bay the apprehensiveness that was making moist her palms and parching her mouth.

Sir Jason Hunter was to be her lover, to know her body as intimately as would a husband. Goose bumps rippled fierily over her limbs in response to the wild images that ran amok in her mind. Although they were not touching she felt intensely conscious of his muscular physique and the clean fresh scent that emanated from him.

She took a glimpse at his profile, acutely conscious of his

silence. Perhaps his odd humour sprung from the fact that he had been the quarry. He had a reputation as a womaniser. Was he a Hunter by name and by nature—a man who liked being a predator? She might have pricked his male pride by audaciously approaching him. That train of thought lead to something else. Perhaps a woman brazen enough to start the chase was expected to bestow an appropriate token of gratitude for her victory. She glanced swiftly about; there was certainly nobody in the vicinity to witness a little wanton behaviour. 'Would you like me to kiss you?' she softly volunteered.

Jason tipped up his head and barked a hoarse laugh at a canopy of dancing branches. 'Of course…though perhaps not here…'

But Helen had already slid dutifully towards him to comply.

She had pressed her body close to his, so close that his thigh felt like immovable rock against her soft yielding flesh. She heard a muttered oath and was lifting her face to investigate what now had vexed him when her jaw was cradled between his palms. That first softly sensual caress caught her breath in her throat. For a lengthy moment their eyes met, then Helen's lashes dropped and she felt his mouth cover hers.

It was so long since a man had touched her in passion that his virility overwhelmed her. His kiss was confident and clever; her mouth was parted and his tongue stroking its silky warmth before she had fully accepted their intimacy. But she participated when he led her to do so. A hand deftly infiltrated her cloak, caressing her midriff through her dress and she curved closer. She felt his thumb sweep the underside of her breast, then extend upwards until it brushed against her nipple. A surge of warmth enveloped her as his hands and mouth worked their devious magic. She felt her head eased back against his arm by the increasing pressure of his kiss. Her lips clung, widened when he urged them to do so and a throb low in her pelvis instinctively made tight her abdomen whilst relaxing her thighs. The core of her femininity felt hot and dewy and a rasping breath was welling in her throat. But within a moment the exquisite tension was ebbing. He had taken up the reins and set the vehicle in motion.

Inwardly Jason cursed Peter Wenham to damnation even as he wryly acknowledged that his friend's inopportune arrival was probably a godsend. He had been on the point of losing control and Hyde Park was certainly not the best place for an al fresco romp with a respectable woman. Helen wasn't a seasoned harlot, she wasn't even right as a mistress, but her sweet seduction had swept from his mind any noble thoughts he'd had of saving her from herself. He wanted her. His loins were afire and, no matter how he strived to be rational, what dominated his mind was finding another quiet place to take her…so he could finish what she'd started….

When Helen observed the smart curricle approaching she was still dazed with heady languor. Slowly she came to vague awareness of the occupants who looked to be a modish young couple. She blinked as Jason and the gentleman acknowledged each other with a word and a nod as the vehicles passed. Then they were out of the park and Jason calmly tooled the horses to a trot on a busy street.

Helen touched two vibrating fingers to her pulsing lips. For her, their first kiss had been unexpectedly shattering, the memory of it consumed her mind. Jason seemed undisturbed by their intimacy and that stirred a peculiar feeling in the pit of her stomach.

The phaeton soon got up quite a speed and Helen pulled her cloak closer about her to ward off the chill of fast-flowing air. Her gloved fingers tweaked her small hat forward to shield her face.

'Are you cold?'

'A little.'

'Grosvenor Square is not far.' A ghost of a smile touched Jason's mouth as he realised that lust had, after all, surrendered to decency. He'd settle for conversation this afternoon. 'We can go there and resume—'

'No.' Her sharp interruption made him arrow a look at her. Her apology was limited to a wavering smile. 'I fear I might be colder still if your butler again shuts me in that cupboard,' she weakly joked.

'That was very bad of Cedric,' Jason said, matching her levity, but his eyes were delving deeper into her brusque refusal.

Helen quelled her misgivings. In fact, she inwardly mocked herself. Had she expected a notorious rake to go into raptures over a quick kiss in the park? Suddenly she felt rather silly to have instigated it at all. He had told her he had done with flirting years ago; clandestine embraces in public places probably provoked in him similar ennui. Inwardly she squirmed for she was never more aware of her lack of womanly sophistication. 'I ought return home immediately. I expect Charlotte will wonder where I am.' Her defensiveness made her sound rather haughty.

'I shan't keep you long at my house.' His tone was adamant and her tawny eyes widened in alarm.

Abruptly he reined back the horses to a slower pace. 'I make it a rule never to ask a mistress to entertain me in my own home, especially not when my sister is in residence. Yesterday she came up from Surrey with her husband.'

'I didn't mean…that is, I know you would not expect…' Helen frowned as she vainly scrabbled to find words to smooth the situation.

'You don't know what I expect, Helen,' Jason softly emphasised. 'And that is one reason why we need to resume our conversation. Had you not distracted me…' he shot her a lightly amused look '…we might have concluded our talk in the park. Another thing we need to speak about is your ulterior motive in all this.'

Helen blushed to the roots of her silky black hair. He sounded as though he was about to accuse her of being a crafty harlot. 'I know you must think me shockingly brazen to proposition you…but I have my reasons.'

'I'm not that easily shocked, sweetheart,' he said on a dry laugh. 'Nevertheless, I'd like to hear your reasons.'

Her wind-parched lips were moistened with a flick of her small tongue. She had not been expecting an inquisition. He knew her husband was dead and that she lived frugally. Surely he could use his imagination as to her motives? She had assumed that, if he desired her, little else about her circumstances would bother him. Perhaps he was used to women hinting at having an uncontrollable *tendresse* for him or flattering him over his handsome looks and social position.

'I have no objection to explaining myself, but I would rather not go home with you and meet your sister. It would be unseemly, when soon we will…' Her explanation faded away.

'Beatrice would remember you as an old friend she has not seen in a long while. As of yet there is nothing unseemly to fret over.'

Helen sank back against the seat. Humiliation stung colour again into her cheeks—suddenly it occurred to her that he might have changed his mind. Perhaps he had been little impressed by her seduction and was trying to wriggle free of his agreement to care for her. A penetrative glance at his profile was not enlightening, but she felt her pride rally. 'If you think you made too hasty a decision and want to reconsider, I would understand and never again mention the matter.'

His muttered oath was inaudible to Helen for her gasp of alarm had filled her ears. Without warning, but with expert skill, Jason had turned the phaeton in the road. Helen found herself clinging to the side of the spinning vehicle that was soon hurtling back towards Hyde Park.

A few minutes later Helen was glancing about to see that the phaeton was stationed in the same quiet spot as previously. The avenue was once more deserted.

He turned to look at her with stormy eyes. 'If we can't go to your house or to mine, we shall need to stop here a while longer. What have I said to make you think I no longer want to sleep with you?'

Helen blanched and slid him a glance that appealed for a little more delicacy.

'Don't be coy about it, Helen,' he said quietly. 'We both know what this entails. I shall provide you with *carte blanche* in return for the privilege of sharing a bed with you whenever I so desire. Or is it that you are only now giving serious thought to the consequences of being my paramour?'

'Of course I have given it serious thought!' Helen cried with stifled indignation. 'If you think I would have lightly humbled myself to proposition you, sir, then you are wrong!'

'Jason.'

Helen glanced at him in confusion.

'My name is Jason. We're now on familiar terms, aren't we?'

'Yes,' Helen breathed. 'Jason.'

He grunted a laugh at her mutinous expression. 'Far from not wanting you, my dear, you've made me an offer I can't refuse. But I need to be sure you understand the ramifications of becoming my mistress.'

'I do understand,' Helen readily affirmed. That brave statement was not entirely true and her mind pondered on latent messages. The more she pondered, the more she was sure their brief kiss had disappointed him and he was implying she might prove an inadequate lover. 'I expect you know I was not married for long. But I am not too unpractised in the passion and pleasure to be had between a man and a woman. I recall enough to—'

'It's not that,' Jason brusquely interrupted. Then added in a soft drawl, 'But thank you for such delightful news.'

'Don't mock me!' Helen's voice held both a plea and a command.

Jason simply smiled and lazily shifted position on the seat. 'I was referring to the impact this will have on your present way of life. When it becomes obvious that you're my mistress, gossip will ensue, although it should not last long. Some of your present neighbours and acquaintances might shun you if feeling fastidious. There will be social events to which it would not be appropriate to take you.'

'I have thought of all of that.' Helen said. She squarely met his grey eyes. 'And in case you are too gallant to mention it so early on in our dealings, I shall say it for you. I know you will tire of me eventually. And even before then I expect you will be reluctant to remain faithful. You need not fear that I will nag or become fretful if you do not devote yourself exclusively to me.'

Jason threaded the reins through his fingers. 'I'm not sure you are suited to be my mistress, Helen. You sound to me like the perfect wife, my dear.'

'I would rather you did not make of it a joke, sir. I am simply trying to be fair and practical.' She had thoughtlessly reverted to using a formal address and it made him quirk an eyebrow at her. 'If I seem calculating, Jason,' she deliberately, stiltedly, used his name, 'I do not mean to appear so. But neither do I want to be accused of being a hypocrite.'

'And what about love and marriage?'

Startled, Helen glanced at him. She had certainly not expected him to bring up any such emotive subject. Briskly she put his mind at ease. 'I promise not to embarrass you with any such declarations or demands.' A private little smile sweetened her solemn demeanour. 'I feel fortunate to have known the love of a fine gentleman. I was a wife just a short time, but I was very happy and have no wish for another husband. I am content with my memories.'

Jason's expression remained unreadable a moment longer, then he gave her a slow smile. 'And what about me? Or perhaps you think love and marriage pass rakes by.'

Helen blushed at that mild sarcasm. 'Not at all, sir…Jason,' she glibly corrected herself. 'I know you have a…lady friend…and I assumed that, if you had a deep affection for her, you would decline to take me in her place.'

'In her place?' Jason echoed so quizzically that further words were unnecessary.

Helen twisted together her fingers. He was starting to needle her, quite deliberately, she imagined. On a deep breath she said, 'I imagined that if you loved Mrs Tucker you would not want to hurt her by giving her a rival.' She was unsure why his response was so important, but found herself awaiting it with bated breath. But he remained uncommunicative and his ruthless gaze made her seek something else to say to shatter the silence.

'I also realise you will one day marry a nobleman's daughter and wish to start your family. I have promised already not to make a fuss when it is finished between us.'

'You have given it a lot of thought,' Jason murmured. 'What makes you think I'll marry a nobleman's daughter?'

Helen did not want to reveal that George had told her of Jason's ambition to marry for pedigree. It might stir more enmity between the two men. She gave a vague shrug. 'It seems sensible to me to conclude that a rich gentleman would choose to do so.'

'It seems sensible to me to conclude that a rich gentleman would not need to do so…unless he was in love with the lady.'

'Are you in love with someone?' Helen blurted.

'I'm not sure,' he answered, seemingly unaffected by her impertinence in asking.

Helen swallowed a lump that had suddenly formed in her throat. She was not so naïve as to suppose that a wealthy bachelor would not keep a mistress simply because he was in love with a débutante. But she felt a fool for not having anticipated that might indeed be the case. He obviously socialised with the best families. 'I'm sorry to pry, but if your affections are engaged and you soon will take a wife, I'm not sure that I—' Helen clamped together her lips for she had been about to blurt that she might not be able to bear it.

'You're not sure how philosophical you would still be about it all?' Jason suggested mildly.

Helen nodded and found she could not look at him.

'If I decide I am in love, Helen, I promise you'll be the first to know. Likewise if I decide to marry.'

'Thank you,' Helen murmured.

'As you have concluded I will tire of you, I take it you have a plan for what to do next?'

Inwardly Helen winced at his ironic tone. Outwardly she gave a single nod. When she could no long avoid looking at him she turned, chin up, to face him.

'And?'

'I will ask you for a settlement. I believe that is not unusual or avaricious in these cases,' she said levelly.

'As we are being very honest and practical, shall we discuss it now?'

The question was equable, almost gentle, but far back in his eyes was laughter and Helen felt her fingernails score her palms. He had the benefit of wealth and security and found her lack of those things amusing. She snapped her head up and gazed into the budding trees. 'I should like the deeds to Westlea House and a sum that I might invest for income…say, one hundred pounds per annum for three years.' She slid him a glance. 'Is that fair?'

'If you're satisfied with that, I'm concerned that I've been vastly too generous in the past.'

'It's enough all I need,' Helen said quickly.

She suddenly felt anxious to be home—she craved respite from his latent mockery. 'I really ought go now. Charlotte has been alone for some time and she is poorly.'

'You were going to tell me your reasons for instigating all this,' Jason reminded her. 'But I dare say it will wait for another day. I'll start to make the necessary arrangements, shall I?'

Helen vigorously nodded whilst frowning into the distance.

He took up the reins, but hesitated in sending leather undulating over the backs of the beautiful chestnut horses. He addressed her without turning his head. 'Just tell me this…did you decide to offer yourself to protect your sister from me?'

Helen swiftly looked at his unflinching profile.

'Tell me the truth. Do you still believe I have nefarious intentions towards Charlotte?'

He was still staring straight ahead and Helen put a light hand on his arm to make him turn to her. 'I'm very sorry I ever was taken in by such a ridiculous tale. Certainly it has no bearing on my proposition.' She glanced down at her lap, for his steely gaze was now upon her. 'You know, of course, that George sowed that seed in my mind. I want to believe his motive was not all bad. I expect he hoped I would persuade Charlotte to quickly marry someone of influence and forget Philip.' She tipped up her head and an involuntary little sigh escaped her. 'George is right in one respect: until she is married Charlotte is vulnerable. She does need a husband to provide for her and protect her reputation. George might be her guardian, but he has no shame in letting it be known she cannot rely on his care.'

'And neither can you.'

'And neither can I…' Helen echoed and turned to look over the lake as the phaeton left the park.

Jason watched Helen slide a swift peek over a shoulder at him before disappearing into the sanctuary of Westlea House.

A rueful smile touched his mouth as he regarded the front door being rapidly closed. Then he set the phaeton in motion, but instead of heading towards Grosvenor Square he turned again towards Hyde Park. For the third time that afternoon he brought the vehicle to a stop in the same spot. It was fast approaching the fashionable hour for the beau monde to parade within the environs of the park. Although strollers and vehicles were more in evidence, Jason sat gazing out over the greensward oblivious to the company.

His brow furrowed with the intensity of his thoughts. Having decided just a short time ago that he would approach Helen Marlowe and offer her his protection, he was not sure why her timely proposition had unsettled him. Certainly he wanted her. Just a ghost of her scent and warmth remained on his clothes from when they had kissed, yet the pulse in his groin was unabated. The torment was keen and, with a frustrated mutter, he bowed his head towards hands that were clasped close to his knees.

He could have approached her some time ago, but had hesitated without giving proper thought to why he was delaying. Now he understood that he had never fully accepted the decision he had made regarding Helen's role in his life. At the back of his mind had always been an idea he might ask her to marry him. Now he didn't know whether he was regretful or thankful that he had kept those thoughts to himself.

Barely an hour ago she had made it perfectly clear that being his mistress was preferable to being his wife. Helen had no wish to remarry, for she was still in love with her dead husband. But she would sleep with him. Not only that, she would not interfere in his life. Nor would she make any demands on him other than he keep her until she had earned the deeds to her home and a sum to scrape by on. And just in case he wasn't convinced that she was seriously prepared to humble herself in such a way, she had attempted to act the wanton.

And it had worked; despite her nervousness, despite him knowing she was simply behaving in a way she thought was expected, he had been enchanted by her artless seduction.

Jason sighed and abruptly tipped up his head to watch clouds travel over cerulean sky. He imagined his conscience was bothering him…or perhaps it was his pride. He didn't believe himself egotistical, but he knew there were several young women of good family and fortune who would be elated to have him propose marriage. Yet an impecunious widow would rather have him as her lover than her husband. If he thought she desired him, it would be easier to bear; but he feared she would tolerate making love with him as she would any other duty to be discharged.

To retain pride and dignity and some control over her life, she had come to him rather than await his approach. Yet despite knowing it all he still wanted her, and inner demons taunted him with the knowledge that, in any case, he could seduce her into lust and after that…why care?

Chapter Eleven

'It is quite beautiful, Charlotte.' Helen swept a thumb across a cluster of rubies adorning her sister's finger.

'Philip just took me to the terrace where we could be private and presented it to me.' Charlotte's eyes glistened with happiness. 'It was enough for me that we were today officially betrothed. I did not expect such a wonderful surprise as this splendid ring.' She wiggled her finger to admire the gem. 'He bought it without any idea what I would like. Yet it is perfect! I could not have chosen better myself.'

'Philip has excellent taste, my love.' Helen gave her emotional sister a soothing little hug. 'One can tell that from his choice of wife.'

Iris Kingston was with her husband, a little way distant from her sisters-in-law, and making scant attempt to mask her boredom. But George had insisted they both attend Charlotte's modest engagement party, held in the prospective bridegroom's drawing room.

Now Iris's expression livened, for she had noticed Charlotte proudly displaying her hand. She sidled closer, manoeuvring into position for a better view of what glittered on Charlotte's finger. A buxom hip was interposed between the slender figures of her sisters-in-law. Snatching hold of Charlotte's wrist, she elevated it to inspect her ring. A disdainful grimace took her plucked eyebrows beneath a fringe of blonde curls. 'It is sweet. But personally I would have expected a love token to be a trifle larger.' Charlotte's arm was released as though it had become hot. Iris flexed her fingers so her jewellery caught candlelight. It was an ostentatious display that shaped her lips into a moue of satisfaction.

Helen fixed feral eyes on her vicious sister-in-law. 'Of course, your build is not so delicate as Charlotte's. Something of less elegance and more substance is needed for a big hand, else there is too much flesh on show.' Helen ignored the glaring blue eyes boring into her; her attention was devoted to admiring her sister's rubies.

Charlotte was too blissfully ebullient to have taken much notice of Iris's cattish remark. Her creamy cheeks were rimmed with excited colour. 'I'm so happy, Helen, I feel fit to burst.'

'Well, I beg you will not!' Helen said with mock alarm. 'Your guests are still arriving. Emily Beaumont is here…and Heavens! It looks to be her brother, Tarquin, accompanying her. I'm sure Emily will be dying to see your wonderful betrothal ring.'

Charlotte pivoted about, her auburn curls jaunty about her shoulders. With a parting smile for her sister, she was soon gliding serenely towards the newcomers, stationed just inside the doors of the drawing room, chatting to Philip and Anne Goode.

Iris peered that way too and a look of distaste puckered her face as she stared at Tarquin, a tall gentleman of about Helen's age with a distinctive shock of flaxen hair. 'I'm sure I have heard about that wastrel,' Iris announced waspishly. 'Is he not the fellow who was lately residing in the Fleet for unpaid debts?'

'Yes,' Helen succinctly confirmed. 'But I do not consider him a wastrel. It is an affliction he has, for he desperately wants to curb his tendency to gamble.'

'What very odd company you sisters do keep.'

'Do you think so?' Helen said. 'Our relatives, then, are probably equally strange. I recall George fretting the duns would have him thrown in debtors' prison. Perhaps he might have shared a cell with Tarquin. But I expect you would have pawned a bauble or two to keep your husband from such ignominy, Iris. Wouldn't you?'

Iris's lips formed a carmine bud. She flicked an encompassing glance about the faded appointments of the Goodes's drawing room. 'It is a nice house Philip has here. Such a pity the interior does not quite match the fine address. One can rarely estimate a person's standards.'

'Philip has done an admirable job in retaining the property and caring for his mother and sister since his father died.' Iris seemed unwilling to let her escape and kept step with Helen as she tried to distance herself.

'A betrothal ball would have been more befitting to people of our standing. This is rather a shabby little affair. But then nothing about this entire episode is *comme il faut.*'

'I agree,' Helen said coolly. 'Were things *comme il faut,* George would have shared the cost of this celebration and not left the entire burden of it to Philip.'

Friends who had come to congratulate the newly betrothed couple were laughing and chatting, creating a buzz of good humour throughout the drawing room. Helen revelled in the atmosphere for a moment, then turned to her sour-faced sister-in-law. 'In this instance, I think I'm grateful for George's parsimony. I'm thoroughly enjoying this shabby little affair…'

Helen's lavender skirts were given an ungentle twitch. 'Ungrateful! George paid for *this* and for Charlotte's new gown.'

'He has certainly taken the credit for doing so, yet I think the sum involved is less than what we are owed in unpaid allowance.'

Iris's complexion glowed beneath her powder. 'And George has been unwisely generous in allowing Charlotte to marry beneath her,' she snapped.

'He has not, for Charlotte is not marrying beneath her,' Helen returned icily. 'Philip is of excellent family. He has had hard times, but his fortunes are now improving. Were they not, I doubt George would even have consented to listen to Philip's suit.' Helen turned to move swiftly on, but bumped straight into George. He immediately held aloft two glasses to prevent the drinks spilling. One was given to his wife and he sipped from the other. 'I ought have fetched you a drink, Helen. Sorry…' he absently remarked.

'You are wasting any such consideration.' Iris gave Helen a significant stare. 'She was just complaining how meanly you treat her and Charlotte.' Iris turned an elevated shoulder on Helen. 'Surely we have done our duty and can now go,' she muttered peevishly to her husband. 'We have been here above an hour already. Sonia Lancaster is having a card party in Hertford Street. It starts late…'

'I'll fetch your cloak.' George watched golden wine swirl in his glass, then speared a look at the doorway. 'That is, if you're sure you don't want to stay and greet our future brother-in-law's patron. It seems he has after all graced us with his presence.' He gave a theatrical sigh. 'I suppose I should make a point of thanking him for easing my burden.' He deliberately slid a look at Helen. 'Perhaps I might yet lose it entirely,' he added slyly. His next comment carried more volume. 'I just hope Goode hasn't frittered the whole of the salary Hunter advanced to him on those rubies.'

Iris immediately swivelled towards the doorway. Her blue eyes took on an excited gleam and she nipped her lower lip between her teeth.

'You don't seem quite so bored…or so keen to leave, my dear,' her husband remarked cynically before strolling away.

Helen deserted Iris too, but walked swiftly in the opposite direction to her brother. Once by the wide doors that opened on to a small terrace she hesitated and let the cool evening air soothe her feverish skin.

Philip had mentioned that he had issued an invitation to his benefactor. Helen had imagined Jason would decline it due to the delicacy of the situation between them. He had made a point of telling her that there would be occasions when it would not be appropriate for them to socialise together. She knew he had been referring to times when their families would be present. Although news of their relationship was not yet out, she imagined he would start as he meant to go on. But not only had he come this evening, he had brought his brother with him, too.

It had been a few weeks since she had propositioned him in Hyde Park and, although they had communicated by letter, she had not again seen him. They had parted, she thought, in an atmosphere of subdued harmony that sunny afternoon. After a few days she had received a letter from him enquiring whether she would like an advance on her allowance. Helen had considered that carefully before putting pen to paper to decline his premature generosity. The following week another missive arrived, asking if she desired choosing her own residence and staff or whether she would want him to deal with it. His mode of writing echoed his wry speech and she had managed a little chuckle on reading his assurance that she could trust him to spare her Rowan Walk. She had dashed off a note to him instructing him to please go ahead.

Certainly they had not exchanged *billets-doux,* but Helen had sensed a fragile amity burgeoning between them. She also had realised the clandestine nature of the prologue to their affair was piquantly thrilling. But, of course, it would not always be just a game, or a secret. At some time they would be lovers, sharing bed and board on occasion, and everybody would know it.

But when? As the weeks had passed, it had occurred to Helen that Jason might be purposely postponing because he was satisfied with things the way they were. He had made it woundingly apparent that Mrs Tucker's services were not to be dispensed with. Had his current mistress got wind of developments and coaxed him to keep the status quo? Once or twice Helen had considered again writing him a note to probe for clues as to the delay, but her pride would not let her. She had humbled herself to proposition him—she certainly would not chivvy him to make a date to sleep with her.

'Charlotte's rubies are beautiful.'

Helen started from her introspection to swirl about in a rustle of lavender satin. Emily Beaumont's eyes were on a level with her own for they were of similar height. She gave the pretty young woman a smile. 'Indeed, it is a magnificent betrothal gift.'

'I'm glad it came right for them both,' Emily said. 'And so expeditiously! Anne told me weeks ago that she feared your brother had taken against Philip and would never give his consent to the match.'

'In truth, I did, too,' Helen wryly admitted. 'But as soon as George learned of Philip's improved situation…well, suffice it to say he has undergone quite a wondrous change of heart. He is keen for them to set an early wedding date.'

Emily cocked her head in the direction of the two distinguished dark-haired gentlemen who stood beneath the room's central chandelier, encircled by a group of people. 'Tarquin tells me Sir Jason Hunter has taken his cousin under his wing and made all this possible. I had no idea that the Goodes were related to the Hunters.'

Helen glanced that way too and immediately noticed that her sister-in-law had lost no time in pressing close to their honoured guest who, she had to admit, exuded magnetism. His dark jacket was excellently tailored in fine raven cloth that enhanced his impressively broad shoulders. The tailcoat was significantly narrower where it skimmed over his lean waist and hips and complemented his grey trousers. He looked, Helen mused, as though his muscular physique owed a lot to strenuous masculine pursuits. An irrepressible image of certain nocturnal exercise had stolen into her mind, making her cheeks warm. She forced her thoughts to fencing and sparring whilst recalling how well toned George had once been when keen to participate in sporting bouts.

'Did you know of the connection?'

Emily's sweet voice infiltrated her mind. She was looking curiously at her…probably to divine the reason for her blushing cheeks, Helen guessed.

'Ah…indeed…I was aware of it,' Helen quickly confirmed. 'It is a distant kinship and one, I believe, that is not widely known, for it has been rather strained in the past.' Her eyes darted again to Jason to see that he was now watching her.

An astute look from Emily veered between Sir Jason and

Helen's quickly averted face. 'Sir Jason seems interested in you. Are you acquainted with the family?'

'Our family lived by the Hunters's estate of Thorne Park…many years ago now,' Helen quickly answered, then neatly evaded answering any more of Emily's questions by asking one of her own. 'I think *I* ought ask whether you are acquainted with the Hunters.' She gave Emily a teasing smile. Helen liked Miss Beaumont. Charlotte socialised more than Helen and so was more of a friend to Emily. But Emily was, at twenty-four, nearer Helen's age. Helen had always thought her a personable and attractive young woman and had wondered why Emily was still single. 'Philip's sister told me that you hanker after Mark Hunter.'

'Cheek! I do no such thing.' Emily's eyes had darkened in annoyance. 'Well, perhaps that's not entirely true. I do hanker after wringing his neck!' Her fair head dipped towards Helen's ebony tresses. 'He is the *gentleman* who set the duns on Tarquin and landed him in the Fleet.'

Helen's amber gaze flicked anxiously towards Tarquin. She certainly did not want her sister's betrothal party ruined by any hostilities. 'I expect Tarquin must feel quite bitter about that,' Helen whispered back.

'But he does not,' Emily spluttered with a perplexed frown. 'Tarquin said a gentleman is entitled to call in his vowels. I think he quite likes him. Heaven knows why! Last time I spoke to Mark Hunter I found him vastly arrogant and—'

'Did I hear my name mentioned?'

That softly ironic query put space between blonde and

black locks. Both young women had snapped their heads up to see a gentlemen smiling at them.

'Mr Hunter…I…it is a very long time since last we met,' Helen said quickly. She politely met his extended fingers. 'And I believe you are acquainted with Miss Beaumont?' Helen exchanged a subtle smile with Emily.

'Of course…Tarquin's sister. I'm pleased to see you again, Miss Beaumont,' Mark said mildly.

Emily refused to touch his hand and slipped into a bob. 'I'm afraid I cannot echo that sentiment, sir. It seems the pleasure is all yours.' Her blonde ringlets rippled as she swung her head to the side. 'Ah, I see Tarquin is beckoning me. I hope he does not already want to go. But his health was not improved by his odious incarceration in the Fleet. He probably feels unwell.' With a smile for Helen and glaring insolence for Mark, Emily was soon on her way.

'Tell me, Mrs Marlowe, am I being overly sensitive or did you also find Miss Beaumont's attitude towards me a tad frosty?'

Helen bit her lip to quell her smile. He shared his brother's sense of irony as well as his striking good looks. 'I believe there is an icicle thawing above your head even as we speak, sir.' More soberly Helen added, 'Emily is very loyal to Tarquin and rightly or wrongly will defend him.'

'I recall you and I dealt together quite well on those occasions you came over to Thorne Park to play with Beatrice. I expect you think I must now be a cruel miser to have had Tarquin imprisoned.'

'I expect Mrs Marlowe is too polite to comment, but Miss Beaumont might have no qualms over giving you your answer.'

Helen turned to see Jason slightly to one side of her. Their eyes coupled for a long moment before he gave her a polite nod. 'It's nice to see you again, Mrs Marlowe, and at such a happy celebration.'

'Indeed, it is a fine occasion, sir,' Helen said rather breathlessly, for her heart had begun erratically pumping. Obliquely she wished she had noticed him approach—she felt silly and girlish to be so discomposed by his sudden closeness. As his eyes lingered momentarily on her mouth it began pulsing beneath phantom pressure. Simply for something to say she blurted on a bright smile, 'But it will be finer still to see them married.'

'Indeed it will,' Jason said softly before his grey eyes were levelled at his observant brother. 'Why do you not go and try to revise Miss Beaumont's opinion of you?'

Mark flicked a glance between Jason and Helen. Suddenly a look of enlightenment flickered over his features. 'Could you not have set me a feasible task, Jay? Reforming Tarquin might be simpler.'

As Mark Hunter moved away Jason strolled closer to Helen, so close that she could sense his heat through the delicate fabric of her new gown.

He leaned back against the wall next to her and she saw him make a sweeping perusal of the company. She had, seconds ago, made a similar swift check to see if they were being observed so understood his scouting look. Only Iris seemed to be darting intermittent glances their way.

'I…it is a long time since I have seen your brother.' Helen made a little light conversation to attempt to curb the fluttering in her stomach. 'I don't think he has changed one bit in looks.'

'Not in looks, perhaps.'

'I remember Mark used to be quite a carefree character,' Helen warmed to her theme and felt relaxed enough to broach the subject of Emily's antagonism towards Mark. 'He has apparently treated Tarquin quite harshly. Does he not like him?'

'Actually, he is fond of him.' Jason slanted Helen a rueful smile before explaining. 'Gambling is like an opiate to Tarquin. Only a true friend would bother to have him forcibly removed from Almack's before he brought himself to complete ruin.' Jason stared off in the direction of where were Tarquin and his sister. 'Mark took away his liberty, it's true, but he also freed him from the tables for a while. Mark has brought a lot of opprobrium down on his head…not least from the Beaumonts. Perhaps they would prefer to watch Tarquin lose his dignity along with the shirt from his back.'

'I hope, then, that it has not all been in vain. I did know of Tarquin's problems, and that he tries to resist temptation.'

'As do we all…' Jason sighed out in a tone replete with irony.

Helen stole a glance at him. His eyes were kindling, making the butterflies in her stomach again take flight. She found another topic of conversation. 'I…it would have been nice to have seen Beatrice this evening. I'm sure Philip intended the invitation be extended to your sister, and her husband, too.'

'I believe they declined due to a prior engagement.'

Helen sensed that was an invalid excuse and suddenly her agile mind pounced on a reason for Beatrice's absence. Immediately she knew she would voice her suspicions whilst they were alone, for there was an opportunity to discover what steps had been taken to make formal her role in his life.

'Has Beatrice chosen to stay away because of…what we discussed in Hyde Park?' It was a leading question she hoped might yield other answers, too.

'As far as I am aware, nobody but us knows about it, unless you have mentioned—'

'I would not!' Helen interrupted in a fierce whisper. 'It is hardly something that I am proud to boast of—' She abruptly bit her lip and her lashes screened her eyes in regret. It was a very unguarded comment to have made.

'Indeed…it's something you're ashamed of, isn't it, Helen?' Jason said softly. 'Which reminds me that I'm still waiting to hear what has driven you to choose such a course of action.'

'And I have said that I will tell you,' Helen returned in an undertone. 'But my sister's betrothal party is perhaps not an appropriate place.' Gathering her skirts in quivering fists, she tilted her head to squarely meet his eyes. 'I think I ought to now circulate amongst the other guests.' Helen managed one step towards the company before Jason moved, blocking from view her fragile form with his powerful height and breadth.

He inclined a little towards her and held out his arm. 'I think this guest deserves just a little more of your time, Mrs Marlowe. Come…accompany me to the terrace. I think we need a little fresh air.'

Chapter Twelve

'I hope you have not simply brought me out here so we might bicker.'

'You may rest assured that arguing with you was the last thing on my mind.'

'Well, that is good news, at least,' Helen said with constrained levity as they proceeded towards the railing enclosing a moon-dappled terrace. Her demeanour became again quite serious. 'I beg you will let me first thank you for helping Philip. Had you not done so...well, I am aware that Charlotte's marriage to him would still be a distant dream.' She gazed up at Jason; although his expression was veiled by shadow, she was conscious of his potent allure. 'Whatever happens between us,' she said huskily, 'I would just like you to know that I will always be grateful to you for that.'

A mere dip of his dark head acknowledged her thanks.

Helen turned to look out over the darkling gardens, her small hands gripping the iron balustrade. 'Did you put in a good word for Philip with George, too? Our brother seems very different towards him.'

Jason leaned on the railing close to her and stared up at the sparkling stars. 'What help I've given is Philip's due: a favour to right a wrong done to his family by mine. My great-grandfather caused the rift between the Hunters and the Goodes when he stole the wife of one of Philip's kin some sixty years ago.'

'But…'

'Hush, Helen,' Jason said softly. 'Your sister is happy; my cousin is happy. There's no reason to analyse how it all came about.'

Helen again started to speak, but he interrupted her with, 'You look very stylish this evening.'

Helen brushed a gloved hand over the sleek lavender satin of her skirt. It was the first time he had seen her well groomed since she was a child. Oddly she felt piqued rather than pleased by his compliment. She rested her slender hips against iron, boldly facing him. 'Why, thank you, sir,' she said with acid sweetness and arranged her gossamer shawl about her shoulders. 'I suppose I ought to have warned you that I do brush up quite well.'

A grunt of laughter preceded, 'Indeed you do. I never doubted it for a moment.' He watched her from beneath lazy lids. 'You always look delectable. But it is the first time in a long while I've seen you in a pretty dress.' He raised a hand to gently cup her sharp little chin. 'I have just one small criticism to make…' A pin was eased from her glossy coiffure and an ebony curl spiralled slowly on to a milky shoulder. 'I like your hair loose…'

Helen gasped and attempted to snatch back the pin to anchor the ringlet again into place. But Jason was not done ruining her careful *toilette*. A thumb leisurely traced over her soft lips. 'And you don't need artifice,' he murmured. 'Besides, it's likely to arouse suspicion if I go back inside sporting rouge.'

'Jason, you mustn't…someone might come…'

An imprisoning arm settled either side of her and Jason brought his head inexorably closer. His mouth tracked hers until, done with half-hearted evasion, Helen turned to him of her own volition. Her lips parted and her eyelids drooped in languid anticipation. After a moment, when all she could sense was his body warming hers and a lemon scent enveloping her, she flicked a glance up at him. She understood the demand in his searing look and immediately complied by going up on tiptoe. About to press her soft lips against the hard contours of his mouth, a bark of laughter made her jump. Immediately one of his hands moved to rest, cool and confident against the silk of her jaw, encouraging her to stay still.

But the moment was lost. Helen jerked back against the balcony whilst peering anxiously in the direction of the doors that opened into the drawing room. Laughter erupted again, sounding disturbingly close. Jason's splendid waistcoat received a little thump as Helen attempted escaping to a respectable distance.

Having first cursed beneath his breath, Jason murmured,

'I've missed seeing you.' He pushed himself back from the railing, allowing her liberty.

'Indeed? You know where I live,' Helen tartly rejoined whilst keeping a vigilant eye on the moving figures she could glimpse between the stirring edges of the curtains.

A smile tugged at one side of his thin mouth. 'That encourages me to think that you've missed seeing me, too.' It was stated with an amount of throaty satisfaction.

Helen bit back the spontaneous denial that had sprung to her tongue. There was no point in acting the coquette. He didn't bother with flirting; she imagined he might also be out of patience with women who feigned indifference to him. With that thought in mind she blurted, 'I was expecting to hear a while ago that you had made certain arrangements. Have you been too busy to give much thought to it?'

'I've thought of little else.'

Helen's eyes soared swiftly to his face. 'Is it all finalised?'

'Why do you want to continue with something that you fear will damage your self-respect?'

Helen was momentarily stunned into silence by his acuity. Then briskly she said, 'I think you presume to know too much about me. If you think I will cry wolf once you have gone to the trouble and expense, I can assure you I will not. I promise you I am at ease with our…new relationship.'

'Are you?' Jason said drily. 'Well, I am not sure that I am.'

'You don't really want me at all, do you?'

He gave a grunt of harsh laughter. 'If that were true it would solve a lot of problems.'

'Then why are you delaying…?'

'I'm flattered by your impatience, my dear. But you did promise not to nag me, Helen,' he drawled in mild rebuke.

Regret and humiliation swept over Helen. She had obviously made herself sound like a shrew as well as a desperate wanton. A cool hand flew to a flaming cheek to gauge how obvious was her mortification.

Jason understood the gesture and with a low imprecation enclosed a fragile wrist with long fingers to draw her comfortingly close.

Helen immediately flung him off. 'If this is a game to you, sir, it is not to me,' she hissed in a low breath. 'If you are content with just Mrs Tucker as your mistress, you only have to say…'

'I want you, dammit, and you know it,' he gritted out in immediate response.

Helen sent a startled look at him, then at the French doors, but it seemed that the people who had stationed themselves just inside had moved away.

'So again I have answered all your questions,' he said with harsh self-mockery. 'I certainly think it's time you answered mine.'

Helen nervously laced her fingers, then just as quickly jerked them apart. 'Very well,' she burst out. 'I shall start by saying that I suspect you find awkward this unforeseen aspect to my character. I am no longer the innocent child you once knew. I suspect also that you would rather I had not propositioned you at all. But I have, and I do not regret it.' Helen gazed boldly at him before her tawny eyes swept away to the velvety blue horizon. A scudding cloud made hazy the moon, deepening the dusk. 'I know our families once were close. My father liked you and was upset when you and George were no longer friends. Perhaps you think that because I am of gentle birth I ought to find a genteel solution to being poor. I expect your conscience would be easier if I were to support myself by finding respectable employment, and apply to be a governess or a companion to a lonely lady. Perhaps I might find a position in a shop.'

Having listed out her prospects, she swallowed and turned to him. 'The truth is, I do not want to do those things. I have had a husband who cherished me and, although we had little money, I had my own household. Even before then I kept house for my papa from when I turned seventeen. In short, I have long been my own mistress, and now I would rather be yours than be despised as inferior by employers who are no better than me.' She clutched again at the railing and watched the silver disc shed its fleecy coat. Her wistful face became bathed in milky light. 'So, you see, my self-respect is more under threat from being good than being bad.'

'I'm the lesser of two evils.'

Helen frowned her regret at the horizon. She had not at all intended that it would sound that way, but, in essence, it was true.

Having read her answer from her expression, Jason swung away. He threw back his head to contemplate the stars, and whether to make light of the blow to his ego. But the poignancy in her quiet reflection had subdued him, made him feel churlish for even considering using flippancy to disguise his wounded pride. How much greater would have been the damage to Helen's self-worth had those fears she'd confided been realised. She had not lied or exaggerated in what she'd described might be her future. Many young women who were poor relations endured just such a miserable existence, sometimes at the hands of their own kin. A sudden surge of hatred for George swayed Jason on his feet.

He thrust his hands into his pockets and looked at her for a long moment. 'You need not resort to being bad, or to being employed, Helen.' With just a hint that she would welcome his proposal he would ask her now to be his wife.

Helen swirled about to face him. 'What would you have me do then, sir?' she snapped with subdued volume. 'You know very well that George has squandered our allowance and is heavily in debt. Would you have me transfer the burden of my keep to my new brother-in-law? He already has his mother and sister depending on him. I need not beg for a home, I know the offer will be freely given. But Philip and Charlotte deserve their privacy and their honeymoon years. I will not live with them.' It was a vehement statement that brought a sheen of tears to her eyes. Helen swallowed the ache in her throat. 'And before you offer it, I do not want your charity. But again I must thank you for your concern. You have recently provided more for Charlotte and me than has our own brother.'

'You ought to marry,' Jason stated more roughly than he intended. 'Harry Marlowe would want what is best for you.'

Helen nodded, a faraway look in her topaz eyes. 'Yes, he would,' she dulcetly agreed. 'And Harry would know that a loveless marriage is not right for me. I would far sooner have my independence and my widow status than a roof over my head and a lifetime of disappointment with a husband who remains a stranger.' She gave him a wry smile. 'Do not fret for my virtue and try to find someone to make an honest woman of me.' A little chuckle escaped her. 'Harry used to say I was too romantic and not nearly practical enough. And so I was.' She glanced at Jason. 'He would be quite amazed at how reversed are now those traits.'

'And what became of your romantic nature?' Jason asked quietly.

Helen cocked her head to one side and held out her hands before her, slowly intertwining her slender fingers. 'Oh, I am still a romantic on occasions…' A sweetly shy smile flitted to him. 'Have you not noticed how enchanted I am by Charlotte's betrothal? She has the most wonderful engagement ring…rubies and diamonds, and soon we will shop for her trousseau and discuss a wedding breakfast and flowers and so on…' She absently rotated her plain gold wedding band. 'Oh, there is still a lot to enjoy that is wonderfully romantic.' Aware suddenly of a quiet protracting between them, Helen neared him and looked calmly into his eyes. 'I have told the truth. Has it put you off having me as your mistress?'

'No.'

She smiled up at him, marvelling again at how extraordinarily handsome he was. 'We have been honest in the past. I like being able to speak plainly to you. I was not nagging you earlier, it is just…'

'You don't want me to ruin your plan.'

'And will you?'

'Of course not.' He smiled at her before dipping his head and taking her mouth in a swift, hard kiss.

Helen was still reeling from that bruising assault when he said, 'At least you consider me the devil it's better to know. I'm not sure everyone would agree with you.'

Helen looked earnestly up into his dark, long-lashed eyes. 'I do not think you a devil at all,' she said with husky sincerity. 'You have been considerate and kind and it will certainly be no hardship to—' She broke off, aware of being a word away from reassuring him with indelicate candour.

'Go on…' He turned her face up to his with relentlessly firm fingers. 'We speak plainly…don't we?'

'It will be no hardship to be intimate with you…to sleep with you.' It was uttered almost defiantly and she boldly held his gaze. 'You are not a repugnant character or physically ugly. In fact, you are quite handsome, as I'm sure you know.' She felt her cheeks warming beneath the sudden glint of humour in his eyes and whipped about her head to frown at the moon.

'Thank you, Helen, for that compliment. And you are quite beautiful, as I'm sure you know. There…in one respect we make the perfect couple,' he remarked drily. 'I think that the theatre or Vauxhall Gardens is probably the best place for our first outing together. Have you a preference?'

Helen swiftly shook her head and murmured, 'No.'

'I'll send you a note detailing what I've arranged,' Jason said. 'I've taken a house on the outskirts of Chelsea that I think you will like. We will finish the evening there, if you're agreeable. I imagine you would want to return to Westlea House and not leave your sister alone at night?'

Helen nodded and chewed her lower lip before sending him a wavering smile. 'It would be best if we are very discreet about our times there, at least until after Charlotte is married and moves in with Philip. I would not want her to be shunned should it all leak out.'

'Of course.'

'Thank you.'

'I think it's time we went inside.' Jason extended a hand to her; their progress towards the French doors was timely, for a couple strolled out. Mr and Mrs Bond were neighbours of the Goodes and they exchanged a few words about the happy occasion before Helen and Jason continued into the drawing room. Without another word passing between them, Jason led Helen towards her sister and ten minutes later politely took his leave.

'What in damnation is *he* doing here?'

Iris swung her blonde head towards her husband, then followed the direction of his astonished glower. 'I invited him.' It was a brisk response, for her china blue eyes had returned to a more fascinating sight than Colin Bridgeman's late arrival at Charlotte's engagement party.

Some fifteen minutes ago Iris had noticed Jason and Helen go to the terrace. She had imagined he was simply being courteous, for Helen had the appearance of being flushed and in need of a little air. But now they were back inside and Helen seemed the opposite of refreshed. Slashes of pink were more vividly highlighting her cheekbones and her eyes were extraordinarily bright. Not only that, her new hairstyle looked in disarray, with tendrils draping about her face. Iris was an expert in the art of covert dalliance in company and could easily spot the signs that betrayed when others had indulged.

Iris narrowed her eyes on Helen's distinguished escort. Of course, Jason seemed unruffled…as ever he did. Iris pursed her lips—insufferable thoughts were pricking at her mind. Had the skinny little drab managed something she so far had failed to achieve and hooked the *ton*'s most charismatic rake? It seemed too incredible to contemplate one moment longer and yet… Helen was a needy widow. Iris looked back to her sister-in-law to make a thorough female assessment. A fierce glint fired in her eyes: the conclusion to which she came was that Helen had the radiant aplomb of a woman who had just secured a wealthy protector.

'You invited Bridgeman to Charlotte's betrothal party? Why, in God's name?'

George's angry demand interrupted Iris's agitated thoughts. 'I deemed it the least I could do,' she exploded in exasperation. 'You virtually implied Colin could have Charlotte as his wife. It is best we smooth things over with him. We do not want to lose his friendship.'

'*I* do,' George said with sour significance. 'You have so many friends, my dear…all gentlemen. Surely you could lose just the one?' George looked past his wife's shoulder to see that the unwanted guest appeared to be making his way relentlessly towards them.

Colin Bridgeman was about George's age, but there ended all similarity. Bridgeman was of average height, fair of complexion with sandy hair. George was tall and swarthy. Colin was thin and favoured peacock colours whereas George was beginning to spread about the middle and dressed quite conservatively.

George had never really liked Colin, but they were old acquaintances and, with few friends between them, he was a ready companion when no better was to be had. Before George married they had gone roistering about town. Now more sedate pastimes of dice and cards, or taking a tipple, drew them together at the clubs.

When he turned thirty, Colin had taken a sizeable inheritance from his grandfather's trust. But years of having little in his pockets had left him close-fisted. Then, recently, George had unexpectedly found a way to prise apart Bridgeman's fingers, and in doing so he had opened a can of worms.

When Colin offered to forward him a loan to keep the duns at bay…and a little in reserve…in return for permission to pay court to Charlotte, George had thought it perfectly acceptable. He was even pleased to think that Colin's approach meant he had not taken offence at having had rejected his quite reasonable offer for Westlea House. Had Jason Hunter not offered handsomely for the property, Colin would be the new owner.

Now George wished he had not taken a penny piece of the man's cash. He would not have done so, he commiserated with himself, had it not seemed that Charlotte's swain was destined to remain a pauper. George had no real wish to see his young sister unhappy, but neither had he any intention of continuing to support her financially. He therefore had decided to be practical. It had occurred to George, and had been an added incentive, that were Bridgeman to marry a woman younger and prettier, his wife might be abandoned by her latest conquest.

In that affair, George exonerated Colin. He had come to accept that it was his wife who instigated her liaisons. Once he would have denied such knowledge, finding it humiliating and distressing. George watched his wife simpering as her paramour came closer and suddenly realised he no longer cared very much what she did.

On the strength of the two men soon becoming brothers-in-law George had thus accepted substantial financial assistance. Rushing to lay hands on the cash, he had heedlessly signed the contract before properly checking the clauses. Now he knew that the rate of interest charged to him was extortionate; not only that, but the loan was also repayable on demand. And he had just that morning received such a demand: Bridgeman wanted his money immediately returned with interest.

Had he realised the precarious position he would land himself in, he would not have given Philip Goode his permission to marry Charlotte. But Jason had made it clear that Philip had his patronage and was destined for success. George might not like Jason, but he was one of the *ton*'s most influential and affluent gentlemen. He had happily pondered on being showered with plaudits for being canny enough to welcome a wolf in sheep's clothing into the family.

George scowled to himself as he saw his young sister laughing with her future husband. Goode might be destined for success, but he seemed destined for disaster! If he could not pacify Bridgeman and wheedle a little time to pay, he might yet find himself languishing in gaol....

'The blushing bride-to-be looks exceptionally charming this evening.'

George gave a well-feigned start as he turned to Bridgeman. 'Colin...there you are...'

'Of course, here I am. I'm sure any betrothal party is not complete without the jilted fiancé putting in an appearance.'

George noted his wife wince at that sarcasm and swiftly steered Colin away a few paces. 'Now steady on, Bridgeman,' he hissed. 'No such arrangements were ever properly made. God's teeth! You didn't even call on Charlotte once.'

'Not for want of trying. Whenever I said I was ready to pay a visit, you told me to wait for your instruction on it. Then you instructed me she was to marry this whippersnapper.' He cast a derisive look in the direction of Philip Goode.

'Her choice, Colin; her choice,' George sighed out. 'A brother can't interfere with the workings of a sister's tender heart.'

'That's not what you said in Hyde Park when you dragged her home and sent the boy off with a flea in his ear,' Colin reminded him acidly. He gave George an estimating look. 'I would say it has more to do with his cousin's money than anything else. You prefer Hunter's coin to mine, just as you did with Westlea House. So be it,' he snapped. 'Give me back mine, together with the interest you owe, and we'll say no more about it.'

George blanched. 'I will repay it as soon as I can, you know that.'

'That might not be soon enough,' Colin said with a gleam of malice darkening his eyes. 'I want it by noon tomorrow or I'll have you dunned.' He cast a look towards where Helen and Charlotte stood centrally within a group of friends. 'Of course, you have more than one sister…perhaps we may yet find a solution…'

George gulped and Colin's profile received a drop-jawed look. '*Helen? You want to marry Helen* instead?' As he digested that thought, his features relaxed into a wondrous smile.

'Marry her? I don't think so. She's past her prime and a might too spirited for what's nice in a wife. But I'll be happy to take her to bed and pay for the privilege.'

Chapter Thirteen

'You want to proposition Helen?'

'Yes.' Another brooding stare sloped from under Bridgeman's sandy lashes at the group of young women chatting together.

George's eyes swivelled nervously as he realised someone might have overheard their shocking exchange. He quickly manoeuvred Colin by the elbow to a safe distance. 'We are men of the world so I am not about to take offence even though the lady in question is my sister,' he rattled off in an undertone. 'In fact, *I* know it for a sensible solution. If she won't find a husband, what's to be done?' His shoulders elevated as far as his ears. 'An informal arrangement with a gentleman is all that's left unless she's content to grow old pinching pennies.' George's brow corrugated in vexation. 'Trouble is, Helen can be damnably headstrong and uncooperative at times.'

'I know,' Bridgeman sourly agreed. He recalled the terse notes he'd received years ago when she'd rebuffed him. He had not thereafter pursued her; his pride would not let him. But he had not forgotten her either, and the lust to possess her was as strong. It was a while since he'd seen her and he could detect some physical changes. Her face was more sharply honed, and her body less curvaceous, yet for him she still held an irresistible allure. Her full rosy lips were presently parted in an appealing smile and hands that seemed pale as porcelain, and equally fragile, were expressively gesturing whilst she talked. As though sensing she was under observation, she turned her glossy dark head and her joyful smile withered.

Bridgeman's fleshy mouth twisted sardonically. She hadn't warmed towards him. She certainly would not have liked the idea of him as a brother-in-law, of that he was sure. But the piquancy of wedding one sister whilst brooding on bedding the other had certainly given him a reason to consider marrying a chit with no dowry.

Colin came to awareness of George curiously eyeing him, no doubt wondering what kept him so moodily quiet. 'I take it she has never told you that I offered her my protection a few years ago.'

George's jaw lengthened almost to his chest.

'She turned me down. It's up to you to make sure she doesn't again do so. There's only so much injury a fellow can take before being inclined to retaliate.'

George looked startled by the unsubtle threat. 'If she won't have you, she won't—there's nothing I can do about it!'

'But you are her brother,' Colin stressed silkily. 'And I have every faith in your powers of persuasion.' He gripped

George's shoulder. 'I'll give you a little time to work your magic. In case you need an incentive to be diligent…' he gave a terse nod at a group of young gentlemen '…why do you not go and ask Tarquin Beaumont how he liked the Fleet?'

Helen settled into comfortable squabs and, stripping off her gloves, her warm fingertips pressed dents into the supple hide either side of her. Her eyes darted about the interior of the coach. Before this evening such a luxurious conveyance had been unknown to her. Realising that her hands were lightly quivering, she clasped them together in her lap.

Many hours ago, when Jason had arrived to collect her in this plush carriage, she had noticed curtains twitching in the houses opposite, yet she had continued to feel quite calm.

But now the evening was drawing to a close and she felt less serenely confident. She swayed on the seat as the coach smoothly negotiated a rut whilst conveying her to Chelsea and a new life as a gentleman's mistress.

They were just a short time from being lovers, but he had not rushed her to leave the theatre and embark on the journey. In fact, she had been the one to suggest they left a few minutes before the final curtain to beat the crush of carriage drivers racing to get the Drury Lane crowds back to the suburbs. She had made the remark like a veteran theatregoer, yet something else had been her prime motivation. She had run the gauntlet of speculative stares when entering the theatre; she had no wish to do so again on leaving it.

But the sly glances and whispers were to be expected, and,

in a way, perhaps it was best to encounter them early on. The sooner the gossip started, the sooner it would be finished. In a few weeks another scandalous *on dit* would be doing the rounds and talk of whether or not Sir Jason Hunter had brought Mrs Marlowe under his protection would be less diverting.

Helen guessed that polite society had not made up its mind if Jason was squiring her because his cousin was marrying her sister or whether his interest in her was more personal. During the intervals those with uncontrollable inquisitiveness had invited themselves in to Jason's box with the sole intention, it seemed, of finding out. Amongst others, whose names she had forgot, Helen had been introduced to Lord and Lady Silverston and Viscountess Montague. Then Lady Mornington and her spinster sister had swept in and begun a bold interrogation. Helen had marvelled at Jason's skill in answering a question without revealing a thing. The twins had thus surged out as the curtain rose on the next act, no wiser about Mrs Marlowe's claim on the eligible baronet's affections than when they had arrived. On the surface everybody *seemed* charming, but Helen had long been adept at spotting insincerity.

Yet, on the whole, she had enjoyed her first outing with Jason. She slipped a glance from under her lashes at the lounging figure opposite. Why was she suddenly feeling awkward and anxious? He had acted no differently towards her this evening than at any other time since they had renewed their acquaintance. Whether shielding her from malicious eyes and tongues or fetching her refreshment, he had been unfailingly courteous and attentive. She had no reason not to trust him to treat her kindly in bed, too. It would be different, of course, to the intimacy she had shared with Harry. They had been lovers in the truest sense of the word. Jason desired her, treated her with respect, but she wanted a little affection, too.

'Is it far?' Helen glanced through the shadows at the gentleman opposite looking to be perfectly at his ease.

'We are nearly there,' he answered and she heard the gentle humour in his tone.

Helen felt warmth flood her cheeks. 'I… It is just I am quite hungry, that's all. Are we dining first?'

'Of course,' he said softly. 'Do you think me an uncouth barbarian?'

Helen smiled at his self-mockery and relaxed a little. 'Not at all. In fact, I was just appreciating how gallant you are. I never doubted that you would do every thing quite properly, sir,' she lightly teased him.

'Well, to prove you wrong, I am about to do something quite irregular.' Slowly he unfolded his crossed arms and held them out. 'Come and sit with me,' he huskily invited.

After a fleeting hesitation Helen relinquished her seat and settled close to him. Immediately a muscular arm came about her and she nestled her head quite naturally against his chest. She could sense the hard masculine lines of his body beneath his fine clothes and the verbena cologne he used was pleasantly soothing. Within a few moments her heartbeat had steadied to a more regular rhythm and, feeling cosy and content, she slipped a hand on to the large fingers resting on his knee. He turned his hand, welcoming her tender touch with a brush of a thumb before his lips also saluted her fingers. Slowly he returned their clasped hands to rest on his thigh.

'People will be whispering about us now, won't they?'

'Yes…'

Helen gave a little sigh and nodded in resignation.

'Have you been worrying about it?'

After a moment Helen said, 'Not really for I can imagine what they might be saying. But nobody knows for sure how it is between us…only us.'

'Has your sister quizzed you over it?'

Helen nodded again and choked a little apologetic laugh. 'As we are speaking plainly, I know you will not mind if I tell you something quite shocking. I am afraid Charlotte is wholly under the impression that your interest in me must be honourable.' She knuckled a laugh into submission. 'I have not had the heart to tell her that her hints about double weddings and so on are wildly far of the mark.'

When Jason remained quiet, she twisted her face up to look at him, fearing he might not, after all, have found it an amusing anecdote. His eyes were blocked from view by an angular jaw that looked dusky enough to need a razor. Helen subdued the temptation to sense his skin graze her palm. Instead she angled her head to see his expression and interpret his mood. 'Are you angry? I would not have mentioned it to you, only I thought…I thought it might make you laugh,' she weakly explained. She swallowed, feeling rather foolish. 'I hope you do not think I have said something to make Charlotte think that…'

'Why would I suspect any such thing? After all, you have made it clear to me that you have no wish to remarry. Have you changed your mind?'

Helen's gaze was locked to darkly gleaming eyes that seemed able to probe her soul. She had loved and married Harry Marlowe; she would never want anyone else as her husband…would she? 'No…of course I have not changed my mind,' she whispered. The denial was out, but with devastating insight she abruptly knew it to be false. There *was* a man she would marry, if only he would ask her…

Obliterating years fell away and she recalled being in her teens and daydreaming of Jason Hunter. Those girlish fantasies had faded when they no longer saw one another and then had extinguished beneath her love for Harry Marlowe. Now she could quite painfully recall sitting on the grass in Surrey pulling petals whilst chanting…he loves me, he loves me not…

'No harm is done. And I don't think it will hurt to postpone dashing Charlotte's hopes, do you?' Jason's voice splintered her poignant reminiscence. 'Once she is a married woman, she might be inclined to see things differently.'

Helen managed a single nod, but her alarming self-knowledge had left her mind reeling and her body weak. She made to slump into the seat by his side to ponder on the discovery that Harry didn't, after all, have sole claim on her heart. But he again drew her against him. He tilted up her face and just before their lips touched she sensed she was submerging in eyes like glittering pools of desire.

Helen felt an exquisite ache low in her abdomen start sapping strength from her limbs, for his mouth was moving on hers with wonderfully erotic expertise. Her cloak was loosened and his fingers skimmed her midriff, trailing fire in their wake. Helen felt her anxieties drift away and abandoned herself to the sensual delight he was bestowing. Slowly a small hand crept up to curl about his nape and when next his tongue slid seductively on her lower lip, she flicked hers to it in welcome.

Jason sensed Helen melting beneath his caresses. She was moulding her body against him and igniting in him profound passion. His kiss became slow and deep, his hands swift and confident. Her bodice and chemise were deftly opened and tantalising fingers stroked over silky warm flesh that instantly rose to fill his palms. Jason's slick lips slid to her throat, to the tender nook at her shoulder, before finally claiming the aching little nub her bowed back begged him to soothe.

His tongue moved with skilful slowness, flicking, touching, circling until Helen felt maddened, delirious with delight, and her little guttural cries seemed to well from deep in her throat.

Jason felt a burst of tenderness moderate his urgent need to immediately possess her, for five small fingers had again intertwined with his to clasp together their hands. Besides which, he had no real wish for their first loving to be quickly consummated on the seat of his coach when they were barely fifteen minutes away from a feather bed and many hours of sensual pleasure. He raised his dark head and eyes like smouldering coals roved over a beautiful face set in rigid lines of desire.

Jason continued to kiss her as he brought together the edges of lace to cover her breasts and marvelled that she could be such an intriguing mix of innocent and wanton.

And that conundrum started unwanted thoughts rotating in his mind. Helen Marlow was a woman who didn't want a husband, but who needed a lover. A perfect paramour...under normal circumstances. But this wasn't normal for him. He was different. He was falling hopelessly in love and he didn't want Helen to be his mistress—he wanted her for his wife.

Her brother's thievery might have precipitated her into finding a protector, but he sensed she would, in any event, have been ripe for seduction. He was reasonably sure he was to be her first lover since her husband, and Harry Marlowe had been dead more than half a decade. There was a raw hunger in Helen that made her pliant and responsive to his touch. He kissed her again with sweetness and felt her immediate thrill of anticipation as to what he might do next.

But perhaps it was not just *his* touch she wanted or needed. He was prepared to marry her, but she might have allowed the first philanderer to call by to share her bed so long as he had a few pretty compliments and enough cash to keep Westlea House for her. Even as the disturbing thoughts tormented Jason he knew them absurd. Helen Marlowe was the antithesis of a vain courtesan susceptible to flattery.

And he would have sworn *he* was not a jealous man. But a savage new emotion was poisoning his mind and defeating his restraint. Deft fingers swept up her skirt to expose lissom milky legs before spreading to explore the sensitive darker skin on the inside of her thigh. His kisses coarsened and deepened, widening her mouth.

Helen's hands instinctively drove between them and she jerked back her head. A reproachful look held his defiant gaze and then, with a sigh, she wound her arms about his neck and lay her dusky head against his shoulder.

With a low oath Jason sank against the seat, a powerful arm anchoring her to his side. His head fell back and his lids drooped low as he realised he had after all proved himself an uncouth barbarian. He'd startled her, yet the residue of sensual languor in her stayed. Glancing down at her, he could see dark lashes fanned on pale cheeks and a mouth that looked slick and swollen and achingly inviting. He forked a tender hand over her chin, a thumb brushing soothingly against her turgid lips. For some reason it was the closest he could come to apology.

He had wanted to savour their first loving in every respect. He had wanted them to share conversation and dinner, and leisurely mutual pleasure. Instead he had acted like a callow youth with a hair trigger. The guilt in him made him feel unworthy to again touch her. He smiled ruefully at shadows moving on the roof of the coach; but he knew he would, for, guilt or no, wanting her was ungovernable.

Helen slowly relaxed beneath the thumb sweeping an arc

softly over her cheek. She knew he regretted losing control, but she was not disgusted to know he could be less perfect and more human at times. Once or twice Harry had loved her swiftly and selfishly, then had sheepishly told her that carnality could tempt a man to savagery.

'It is as well it is too dark for me to see the sight you look with rouge smeared on you,' Helen lightly teased. As she sensed rather than saw him lift a testing hand to his face, she giggled, shattering the tension between them.

Jason dropped a kiss on her sleek crown of hair before chuckling, for he had just recalled that earlier that evening he had complimented her on refraining from using it. In a voice of velvety roughness he said, 'I'm sorry….'

'I…I am sorry….'

'It is forgotten,' Jason glibly lied and eased her head down against his shoulder.

Helen immediately sprang up again and a cascade of ebony hair caped her nude white shoulders. She looked down at the handsome dark face starkly outlined by a pristine pillow. She had ruined everything. And it had been so perfect between them up till a few moments ago…

The townhouse to which he had brought her was cosy and elegant. They had enjoyed a delicious meal served up by footmen who flitted discreetly to and from a candle-lit dining room. The grand table had been decked with the finest crystal and china and gleaming silverware. A warm atmosphere that owed little to the blazing logs in the grate had blossomed between them. Helen had felt her inhibitions and her nervousness melt beneath the pleasure of just being with him. When eventually they had eaten their fill and talked into amicable quiet, Jason had asked if she would like yet to go upstairs. It had seemed the most natural thing in the world to agree, and a young maid had shown her to a magnificent bedchamber in which reposed a vast four-poster.

Helen had gently declined the young woman's offers of assistance in preparing for bed. She had wanted time alone; not only to make herself ready but, like a child on a fascinating excursion, to explore her surroundings.

She had brushed velvet bed-hangings with reverent fingers, taken puffy pillows from the bed to peer beneath at the silky white sheets. And then she had found the gossamer negligee draped on a chair beside a dressing chest that held a selection of oils and perfumes and silver-backed brushes.

Helen had tested a scent in a pot on a wrist, wondering if it was the perfume that had wafted in Mrs Tucker's wake on the day she had seen her alight from her stylish carriage. She had accepted, with a twinge of melancholy, that Jason was probably as generous to all his mistresses, but nevertheless she had appreciated being treated well. And now she had ruined everything…

She touched a finger to his face, feeling the stubble on his jaw. She wanted him to open his eyes. 'Please look at me. I…it is not nothing. I would not have liked it at all if you had…I mean, if you had called me Diana at such a time I would have been insulted.'

Jason gazed up at her. 'I'm not likely to do that, *Helen.*' Her name carried a certain stress that told her his nonchalance was poorly feigned.

As though he read her knowledge and it irked that he had betrayed himself, he swiftly turned, drawing her down and beneath him. Slowly he linked brown fingers with white then carried their clasped hands to where the black silk of her hair tumbled over snowy pillows.

'I said it doesn't matter, Helen… Shall I prove it to you?'

Helen felt an odd surge of tears clog her throat, for indeed she wanted him to.

Earlier Jason had made love to her with a skill that had transported her to a level of sensation unknown to her. With a poignant ache she understood how he had acquired such expertise. Diana Tucker, and numerous other women who had come before her, had also gasped and cried out beneath such lavish sensuality. But, when teetering on the brink of explosive tension, had they all remembered to rightfully name the man who had so inflamed them?

Her late husband might not have loved her as slickly as Jason, but such tenderness had existed between her and Harry that they had communicated softly even at the height of passion. And this evening she had called his name again….

Chapter Fourteen

'How much longer are we to endure this?'

The petulant demand snatched Helen's interest from the pearly silk slipping beneath a sensitive palm. 'What is the matter, dear?' she asked Charlotte.

Charlotte shot a fierce look to the other side of the shop's counter. 'They are talking about us, I'm certain of it.' Charlotte gave Helen a glimmering look. 'Or rather, they are gossiping about *you,* I suspect.'

Helen glanced at two fashionable young women who were peeking in their direction. Curious eyes were intermittently visible between the filigree edges of Brussel's lace suspended from rolls shelved on high. Linking arms with her sister, Helen urged her to move on towards the selection of velvets at the other end of Baldwin's Emporium. 'They will soon grow bored and find somebody more worthy of their snooping.'

'I doubt it!' Charlotte announced pithily. 'Sir Jason is very eligible and handsome and the débutantes will naturally want to know whether or not he is taken.' She gave her sister an arch glance. 'I have to say, Helen, I think it is time your beau gazetted a notice.'

Helen felt her cheeks prickle with warmth, but said levelly, 'Sir Jason is not my beau; he is simply a good friend of mine. I have said that you must not hope—you certainly should not say to anyone—that there is more to it than that.'

'Sir Jason intends there be more to it than that, I'm sure,' Charlotte flatly opined. 'He has been calling on you and escorting you around town for two weeks. Everyone has noticed how taken he is with you. Emily and Anne are so excited! Anne has already hinted at how nice it will be to welcome you as a new cousin. She quite thinks of the Hunters as family now, you know.' Charlotte slid a significant look back at the gossiping ladies. 'Not everyone will be so thrilled, of course. But I shall be most surprised—and disappointed—if soon you are not sporting a huge betrothal ring.'

'*Charlotte!*'

Charlotte was unperturbed. 'I'm not so innocent and naïve that I'm ignorant of what people imagine is going on between a rakish gentlemen and a young widow…who happens to be my sister,' she added primly. She gave a cautioning nod and set her auburn curls to bouncing. 'Especially when it gets out how very generous your admirer has been in providing comforts for us at Westlea House.' Under the pretence of examining a bolt of blue velvet, Charlotte stole a peek to see if others found them noteworthy. 'I've no doubt Sir Jason has his pride. He is probably waiting for a little sign from you before he proposes. You must encourage him, or you only have yourself to blame if people start making up lies about the two of you!' Charlotte gave her elder sister an extremely old-fashioned look before taking a more genuine interest in selecting fabric for her trousseau.

'That colour would suit you,' Helen said, desperately bright, as she attempted changing the subject.

'I know you're in love with him,' Charlotte breathed insouciantly whilst trailing her fingers over plush gentian pile.

Helen dropped her eyes to the cloths and in agitation yanked a length of apricot velvet off the roll. But in her mind rotated thoughts far removed from a new gown.

Charlotte was correct in one respect: Jason's generosity had altered her routine and her spending. Obviously it had been noticed that she shopped more and that clue, coupled with her outings with Jason, had naturally aroused speculation that they were more than friends. She was not extravagant, but neither could she mix in polite society dressed in her old clothes. New stockings and gloves had just a short time ago been unaffordable luxuries. She could now purchase a dozen bonnets at a time should she so wish.

George, of course, knew that her upturn in fortune was not the result of his conscience finally troubling him. In fact, she was most surprised that her brother had not been by to express his gratitude that she had found a man to support her.

And, indeed, she was being lavishly supported. She had received a note from her bank of the astonishing sum that had been credited to her account. Her monthly allowance from her lover was more than her sweet papa had estimated his daughters could comfortably live on for a year.

So her plan for her future security was a success: she had acquired a gentleman to keep her, and a promise that in the future Westlea House would be hers. Charlotte was shortly to be married to Philip, who now had excellent prospects. Jason Hunter had within a short time bestowed so much. She had got what she wanted, she again impressed on herself as she absently wandered between rolls of jewel-coloured cloth. For the first time in many years she felt pampered and attractive. Jason treated her with respect and, if not prone to display overt affection, she was sure he was fond of her. He invariably complimented her on her new gowns when he came to collect her from Westlea House. But his patient, polite socialising for a few hours could not mask the fact that he'd sooner go to Chelsea and see her naked. His desire for her was as yet undiminished and sharing a bed and mutual pleasure was her bittersweet role… But he had promised to tell her if he fell in love, or was ready to wed, Helen poignantly reminded herself.

She glanced up and saw the débutantes had not yet conquered their inquisitiveness. At first she ignored them, but then could not help but wonder if either of those pretty young women might capture Jason's heart. He was now thirty-five and, although no further mention had been made between them of his marriage, she knew he must want eventually to settle down with a wife and raise his family.

'Let us go, Charlotte.' Helen abruptly turned to her sister, making Charlotte frown enquiringly at her. 'It is quite warm in here,' Helen excused her need to avoid the nubile young ladies. 'Let's go to the tearoom. We can return here later for another browse.'

Charlotte smiled agreement and linked arms with Helen.

They had barely put a step on to the pavement when Charlotte let out a groan. 'Oh, no! Iris is coming this way with that Bridgeman fellow. We will never manage to dodge her.'

Helen squinted into the glaring sunlight and a sigh of disappointment escaped her, too. Iris had seen them and obviously had no intention of walking on by. Her buxom silhouette was looming at them through the incandescence. Helen blinked and saw that her sister-in-law was dragging her escort along by the arm.

'We're doomed to speak to her, I'm afraid,' Helen muttered to Charlotte just before Iris and Colin Bridgeman came to a halt in front of them.

Iris's blue gaze ranged quickly over Charlotte before sharpening on Helen. 'Have you not bought anything?' she demanded, looking significantly at the sisters' empty hands.

'No…we have not…' Helen began.

Iris let out a shrill giggle. 'Heavens! You have much to learn!' she amiably sneered. 'With such a *friend* as you have acquired, surely you must be able to find something in Baldwin's on which to spend his money?'

Helen felt her cheeks sting and noticed that Charlotte had blushed bright red.

'I expect Mrs Marlowe is a lady of certain taste who likes

to take her time before making her decision,' Colin purred into the tense quiet. 'Sometimes waiting makes possession the sweeter…do you not think, Mrs Marlowe?'

Helen gave him an icy glare, uneasily aware of the insinuation in his tone. 'We were just going to Millie's Tearoom,' she clipped out. 'Good day to you,' and, with a curt nod, she made to propel Charlotte along by the arm.

Iris was not about to lose her quarry so easily. 'I should like some refreshment.' She began to determinedly trail in their wake.

'There's George.' With a relieved sigh Charlotte waved urgently at their brother. He was making slow progress in his carriage for there was a press of vehicles in the street.

George saw them and steered the rig to the kerb then nimbly alighted. If he resented seeing his wife arm in arm with her lover, he gave no sign. In fact, he tried to avoid meeting Bridgeman's eyes at all. When eventually their glances collided, an unspoken message passed between them. George was first to look away and he immediately turned his attention to his sisters.

'Where are you two bound?'

'We were going to take tea in Millie's Rooms, but I think we shall instead go straight home,' Helen said.

Charlotte nodded her agreement to aborting their shopping trip.

'Well, I was just on my way to Westlea House,' George said. 'I'll take you home and save you the hackney fare.'

'I don't think Helen is now short of such a paltry amount,

do you?' his wife sourly muttered. Iris was annoyed at George's interference, for she saw the chance slipping away to interrogate Helen.

George barely looked at Iris. He proceeded to help his sisters alight.

When they had been journeying west for a few minutes, Charlotte asked idly, 'Was there a special reason for your visit to see us, George?'

'Yes,' he succinctly replied after a momentary silence. 'And I won't say more on it till we are indoors,' he finished ominously.

Once back home and in Westlea House's parlour, Charlotte stripped off her bonnet and gloves and lobbed them on to the table. She sank wearily into the sofa. 'A wasted afternoon!' she peevishly complained. 'I feel too cross about it to go to Vauxhall this evening,' she dramatically threatened. 'Why did we not stay in the shop? I could have bought the blue velvet for my honeymoon outfit.'

'If things don't come right for me, you won't need a trousseau; leastways, not for a marriage to Philip.'

For the duration of the journey home Helen had sensed that George was in a fit of the sulks brought on by self-pity. From that she had deduced that he probably had got himself into more financial troubles. But she had not expected him to sink low enough to use Charlotte's happiness as a bargaining tool. And she was sure he was about to reveal a plan.

'You have no right to say such a thing!' Helen sharply rebuked him, for Charlotte's face had turned chalky on hearing his muttering. 'You have given your consent to Philip and cannot now retract even if you have got yourself into another muddle.'

'I would not get into muddles at all if it were not for you two leeches!' George snapped defensively. He paced back and forth, ignoring the withering look Helen shot his way.

'Well, you might as well say what you must,' Helen urged in exasperation. 'You obviously have something unpleasant on your mind. What is it?'

'*Who* is it is what you ought to have asked me.' George brought a fist down on the mantelpiece. 'Damnation! If I had known that Goode would eventually cosy up to Hunter, none of this would have come about.'

'You're talking in riddles, George. What have you done?' Helen insisted on knowing whilst keeping an eye on her sister's fearful expression. Charlotte was batting glances between her and George as though trying to estimate the course of an, as yet, unspoken debate.

'I borrowed money from a fellow to pay off the worst of my debts on the understanding that I'd permit him to marry Charlotte.'

Helen snorted in outrage. Quickly she put a comforting arm about her sister's shoulders. 'Well, that was an astonishingly stupid thing to do—you must have known that Charlotte would refuse him.' She suddenly turned a disgusted look on George. 'It was Bridgeman, wasn't it?'

Charlotte burst from her sister's embrace and, fists

clenched, confronted her brother. 'I would rather run away than have that weasel for my husband.'

'Fortunately he will consider another solution…' George said so hoarsely the words were almost inaudible.

Helen frowned until George's uneasiness and downcast eyes gave her a blinding insight as to what the *solution* was. Her eyes grew round with horrified disbelief. Turning swiftly, she instructed Charlotte, 'Ask Betty to make some tea, please.' She gave her sister a reassuring smile. 'This foolishness will not affect your wedding plans. George must sort it all out.'

Charlotte backed towards the door. 'I swear I will run away if you even say that scrawny coxcomb can call on me!' she shouted at George before rushing from the room.

Once sure that Charlotte was out of earshot, Helen announced tightly, 'If you think I will in any shape or form contemplate a relationship with Colin Bridgeman, you are addled in the wits.'

George gripped the mantel with both hands till the knuckles showed bone. 'I am in serious trouble this time,' he obliquely wheedled for her to reconsider. 'Bridgeman isn't a piddling merchant, waving his invoices. Contracts were signed and he immediately wants back his money.' George looked forlornly at Helen. 'He'll set the duns on me. I might be in the Fleet as soon as next week.'

'How dare you try and prick my conscience. All of this is your own fault!'

George hung his head between arms braced on the mantel.

A sudden sound stopped Helen from quitting the room. She spun about, but did not retrace one pace. She addressed her snivelling brother from the threshold. 'How much do you owe him? I have some cash in the bank…'

'Four thousand pounds,' George immediately supplied the figure in a gurgle. 'Plus some interest, too…'

Helen repeated the amount in disgust.

George made an instant recovery. He pushed away from his support and swiped a hand over his eyes. 'Don't lecture me!' he spat irritably. 'You're hardly Madam Virtue, are you?'

Helen's complexion became grey with rage—she knew to what her brother referred, just as he intended she would. 'No, I'm not,' she whispered. 'I'm what you made me. You forced me to support myself and I am doing so. Your schemes worked. You have Father's money all to yourself, just as you intended, and now you have the outrageous cheek to moralise.'

'How much might you be able to loan me?' George plaintively asked.

'I have at the moment just over one thousand pounds…'

'It is not enough!' George despairingly shook balled fists at the parlour's cracked ceiling. 'Besides, I suspect Bridgeman wants you more than his cash.' He speared a glance at Helen. 'Why did you not tell me that he had approached you before?'

'Because I knew you would try to bully me to accept him, just as you are doing now.'

George looked affronted. 'I've only ever wanted you to be practical. You're not a blushing virgin, after all. And Colin is not such a bad chap. Would you not…once or twice…?'

Helen said icily, 'No, I would not.'

George resumed his pacing about the room, frowning at ceiling, door and wall. Suddenly he halted and spun to face Helen, a grin splitting his face. 'Of course! Hunter would advance you more if you ask him. He is renowned for being generous to his women. You could find a romantic little spot in the Pleasure Gardens this evening and ask him nicely for me.'

'I shall do no such thing, for he has been more than generous thus far,' Helen said in a cold, quiet voice.

'So you will not help me? You refuse to do a thing,' George whined.

'What I *will* do, when next I see Bridgeman, is tell him exactly what I think of him. I'll see if Betty has made the tea.' With that Helen quit the room without a backward glance.

'You're quiet this evening.'

Helen slanted Jason a faltering smile as they promenaded the Long Walk in Vauxhall Gardens. 'I have been engrossed in Charlotte's wedding plans, that is all.' She pressed a little closer to him to indicate she was content. 'Shall we go back and find Philip and Charlotte? The music must soon be due to start.'

As they turned on the path to retrace their steps, Helen's thoughts were once more occupied with her family's troubles.

Before they left the house earlier that evening, Helen had

tried to pacify her sister. Persuading Charlotte that no good would come of relating George's sorry tale to Philip had not been an easy task. But Helen was sure it would be best to keep the matter private. Although he was a placid gentleman, Philip might take it into his head to act manfully to protect his fiancée. Gossips were already having a fine time at Helen's expense. It would not be prudent to give them something new to crow over and risk a stain on Charlotte's reputation.

Helen glanced at the tall gentleman at her side. An aura of power seemed to emanate from Jason and she was tempted to confide her worries. If she asked for money, he would give it to her. But such a sum would beg a question and she had no wish to lie. Neither did she intend disclosing that her brother was venal enough to sell one or other of his sisters to Bridgeman to keep his liberty. Her continuing loyalty to George seemed wasted, as did attempting to shield him from Jason's disgust. But a stubborn scrap of caring seemed entrenched in her soul.

The peacefulness of the Long Walk receded as they neared a more populated area of the Pleasure Gardens. Helen glanced up and sensed her blood freeze. Not more than twenty yards away she spied Bridgeman's thin profile, his mouth agape in a grin. He was with George and some other fellows. A little further on was a party of young people grouped about Charlotte and Philip. Should Charlotte panic at the sight of him she might yet cause Philip to confront Bridgeman.

'I didn't know George was coming here this evening,' Helen

breathlessly said, urging the muscular figure at her side to accelerate his step.

'Are you so keen to see him?' Jason drily asked and took a look down at Helen's countenance, now puckered in anxiety.

'No,' Helen muttered. 'In fact, I wish he and his friends had taken themselves off elsewhere this evening.'

Jason caught Helen to him and gently turned her about. Although her body faced his, her amber eyes were immediately looking over her shoulder. She anxiously eyed the group of gentlemen lounging against a supper box in which were several attractive ladies. 'What's the matter?' Jason asked. 'You have been preoccupied since we arrived.'

Helen sensed Jason's strengthening concern and gave him a wobbly smile. 'It is nothing, really… George upset Charlotte this afternoon,' she blurted in explanation. 'It might be as well to keep them apart. I shall just go and warn her he is here.' Helen looked into a darkly handsome face. A slight lift at a corner of Jason's mouth did little to convince her that he was satisfied with her answer.

'Your brother is heading this way.' Helen's dusky head briefly nodded to the left as she noticed Mark Hunter's distinguished figure weaving towards them through the crowd. 'I shan't be more than a moment,' she said, slipping her hand from Jason's elbow and darting towards Charlotte.

'I don't see anything of you in an age then, delightfully, we meet by chance twice in one day.'

Helen gasped and twisted about to see Colin Bridgeman's

pale blue eyes on her. About to nod and immediately hurry on she hesitated and haughtily faced him. She had told George earlier that she would tell this man what she thought of him. Perhaps now was the perfect opportunity to do so.

Chapter Fifteen

'*I*s it a chance meeting?' Helen bluntly demanded to know.

Colin Bridgeman's bulbous lower lip protruded in amusement. 'I see you're a lady who knows when not to act coy. I like that.' He eyed her appreciatively from beneath stubby lashes. 'I take it from your attitude that George has revealed he is heavily in debt to me. Do you understand how perilous is his predicament?'

'Indeed I do, sir,' Helen breathed in a voice made virtually inaudible by wrath.

'He is a hair's breadth from a stay in gaol. But I can be persuaded to be lenient…did he tell you that?' Bridgeman asked whilst his eyes lowered to Helen's pert bosom, and his wet tongue crawled on his lips.

'He did tell me that. And I will relate to you my response. I have no intention of saving him by becoming your harlot.'

'You'd rather remain Hunter's whore, would you?' Bridgeman's top lip lifted in a sneer. 'That's what people are calling you…did you not know?' he enquired with mock surprise.

Helen swallowed and glanced about, her face white and strained. 'Other than to let you know I despise you, I have nothing more to say to you,' she whispered hoarsely and took a step away from him.

'And *I* have nothing more to say to you,' Bridgeman echoed carelessly. 'Now I think on it, I'd sooner speak to your sister. Charlotte is younger and has the full figure I like. I'll warrant the sweet maid is more tenderhearted where her brother is concerned, and anxious to keep him from the Fleet.' His pale eyes swerved to slyly study Charlotte. 'A virgin, too…' he reminded himself, but with sufficient volume for Helen to hear.

'You will leave my sister alone!' Helen fiercely gritted out. Bridgeman simply winged a ginger eyebrow at her, and made to strut in Charlotte's direction. Helen blocked his path. 'You will not bother Charlotte! She is betrothed and is soon to be married.'

'Betrothals have been broken before when a family crisis demands it.'

Helen darted a furtive look about to see if they were drawing attention. Her golden eyes pulled to the spot where Jason and his brother had been standing, but they had gone. Next she glanced in Charlotte's direction and was relieved that her sister still seemed happily oblivious to Bridgeman's presence. George appeared to be flirting with a young lady in the pavilion upon which he was still supported, negligently, by an elbow.

Helen's attention moved to the odious man close to her and for a moment she simply glared at him. She didn't want to spend another minute in his company, but she feared he was not bluffing. Should Bridgeman carry out his threat to approach Charlotte so soon after her hysterical outburst this afternoon, chaos was likely to ensue.

Sensing her imminent capitulation, Colin purred, 'Come, my dear, we ought not be bad friends. Let us take a little walk along the paths and be free from prying eyes. It will only take a few minutes more to establish if we might arrive at a mutually acceptable arrangement.'

About to reject his suggestion out of hand, Helen hesitated. There was scant chance of them finding common ground. Nevertheless, going with him would prevent him bothering her sister and might even, if she was astutely eloquent, gain George some time to pay up. She allowed her hand to hover above his sleeve—the idea of touching him was repugnant. A moment later a graceful raven-haired woman and her dandified escort could have been mistaken for a couple out for a romantic stroll as they merged into the shadows on the pathway.

Helen's hope that they had departed unseen was far from realised. In fact, several people had noticed her slip away with Colin Bridgeman, and reactions to their disappearance were varied.

Charlotte had been sharing a joke with Emily Beaumont when Emily suddenly began frowning over her shoulder. Charlotte had turned to see what interested her friend and had been agitated to see her sister with the horrible man who wanted to usurp Philip as her husband.

George had also been keeping a sly eye on the proceedings between his sister and his main creditor. His heart had soared as he saw Helen take Bridgeman's arm. But it was short-lived euphoria; his conscience began to worry him at about the same time he noticed the disquietingly saturnine demeanour of the imposing fellow a few yards away.

Jason had moved towards the orchestra podium to greet Peter Wenham and some other friends, but had nevertheless kept an eye on Helen's progress towards her sister. From the moment Bridgeman had intercepted her, Jason had been ready to intervene if necessary.

Helen was an independent woman and Jason was not a character to stalk a mistress and be thought overly possessive. Nevertheless, at one point, when Helen seemed flustered, he had started towards her. A moment later he retraced that step, for Helen had moved very close to Colin before glancing about as though to check they were unobserved. She had obviously felt reassured by her furtive survey—he'd watched relief smooth her brow as she took Bridgeman's arm. There was no doubt in his mind that she'd gone willingly with him into the dark.

Jason had never liked Colin Bridgeman. Since Mark had told him of the incident when Kingston had humiliated Philip in Hyde Park, and Bridgeman had found it amusing, he liked him even less. The man was renowned to be callous and lecherous.

Jason accepted he was hardly fit to judge, for he had long been ruthless in business and predatory with women. But if recent events were anything to go by, he was in danger of becoming not only a reformed character but content with his mellow persona.

Thus he stood for several minutes more, surrounded by his jovial friends, attempting to control the gnawing jealousy he felt. Helen had every right to promenade with her admirers and flirt with whomsoever she pleased. She had promised him nothing more than her body in his bed and that she would not interfere in his life. And she had been true to her word. If she cared what he did, or whom he saw, those evenings they were apart, she gave no sign. It had never occurred to him that perhaps he ought ask what *she* did whilst he sat quietly at home, thinking of her.

Abruptly he excused himself from his brother and his friends and strode towards the walkway. As he passed George Kingston, their eyes briefly met before George shifted his gaze. The wine within George's fist was so abruptly upended into his throat that, some distance on from him, Jason could still hear him choking. A humourless smile tugged at Jason's tight lips. George had looked guilty and if there was any skulduggery afoot, George was certain to be embroiled in it.

Thus, some minutes after Helen and Colin Bridgeman disappeared, Jason did, too.

'I think we have come far enough, Mr Bridgeman.' Helen's fingers recoiled from proximity with his hairy knuckles and swiftly she removed herself to a spot some distance away. The pretty globe lamps swayed high up in the hedge, illuminating the rustic bench framed by an arbour. 'I have but a few minutes to spare, then must return or I will be missed.'

'Come…let us be seated,' Bridgeman coaxed whilst sidling close.

Helen immediately evaded him and moved the other side of the seat. 'I must first ask you to please show my brother a little tolerance. George told me that he was negligent in checking the terms you offered when you made him the loan. Had he wholly understood the document—'

Colin interrupted her with a theatrical sigh. 'You do George no kindness in making him sound such a fool, my dear.' He took a surreptitious step, then another, craftily penning Helen into a corner of yew. 'Do *me* a little kindness, however, and I promise it will pay dividends for that doltish brother of yours.'

'I have made myself clear over that,' Helen reminded icily. She attempted to dodge behind the bench, but it was set too far back into greenery to permit her to escape both him and injury. 'I will never sleep with you.' She put up her chin, intrepidly confronting her persecutor. 'So, if you have no sensible arrangement to offer, you are wasting my time.'

'But *I* think my arrangement is sensible,' Bridgeman cooed. 'And perhaps when Hunter is finished with you, you might not be so precious over it all.' He grinned as he saw her reaction to that. 'I know your rent at Westlea House is waived courtesy of your trips to Chelsea.'

Helen nipped her soft lower lip between her teeth.

'Ah…I see you thought nobody wise to your little love-nest.' Colin's eyes glowed with satisfaction, for he understood what provoked her stricken expression. 'I made it my business to find out,' he admitted with a flick of a limp wrist. 'I followed you there when you and Hunter left the Beaumonts' *musicale*. Extreme tactics I'll own, but that's how you affect me, Mrs Marlowe. I want you and, now I know you're not too prudish to be bought, I will have you.' He eyed her, his head cocked in consideration. 'I could soon ensure the drawing rooms are abuzz with details of how you earn your keep.' He chuckled lewdly. 'I know you don't stare at ceilings in Chelsea every night. On those occasions Hunter prefers the company of a blonde, *I* could take his place.' He hooted in derision. 'Don't look so melancholy, my dear. Did you not know that Diana Tucker is still firmly ensconced in one of his houses?'

Helen felt her throat throb in anguish, but nevertheless whispered, 'My brother is less of a fool than are you if you expect me to stay longer and listen to your—'

Her scorn was not fully expounded, for, with surprising strength and agility, Bridgeman suddenly leaped the space between them, forcing Helen back against the hedge. His moist mouth pounced on to hers and a few fingers delved forcefully into her bodice.

'Am I intruding on a tender moment?'

Colin pivoted about on hearing that glacial sarcasm. His chest was heaving with exertion and thwarted lust. A foul curse scratched his throat; next came a gasp of triumph as he identified the silhouette in the gloom. 'I think you ought ask the lady that…or judge from what you saw with your own eyes, Hunter.' He leered at Helen's shocked countenance.

'Will you tell him about our tête à tête, my dear, or shall I? He will know it all soon enough, in any case.'

Snapping free of her daze, Helen pushed past Bridgeman, the back of a shaking hand wiping the residue of his slimy kiss from her mouth. She took a few faltering steps towards Jason, gazing up appealingly into his shadowy face. He was smiling at her, she glimpsed a gleam of white teeth, but it was his lack of comfort in words or deed that turned her heart to stone. 'It's not what it might seem,' she whispered. 'I…I hope you do not believe I wanted him to kiss me.' Still he said nothing, and she knew that his silence stemmed from a suspicion that she had been enjoying Bridgeman's nauseating attention.

Anger and hurt mingled in her, churning her thoughts to nonsense. But one vital fact surfaced to again torment her: Diana Tucker still figured in Jason's life.

So many times she had been tempted to ask Jason about her. Pride had kept the words locked in her mind, as had the memory of her naïve vow not to pry or to nag or to demand his fidelity. She had thus taken comfort from her certainty that she would *know* if he slept with another woman. Although he did not see her every night, she had convinced herself that the passion and affection they shared was special and fulfilling. When making love he was tender and patient, even when self-imposed duress corded his muscles and betrayed that he would rather plunge headlong to his own release.

Invariably their parting kiss outside Westlea House would be followed by her sound sleep, not simply got from sensual satiation, but from the tranquillity of knowing their intimacy sprang from them being friends as well as lovers. Now she knew how badly she had misjudged the reality.

She sensed that, despite Bridgeman's malice, he had not lied about Diana being still under Jason's protection. Her dream that they might build a future together had been shown as a silly fantasy, not just by knowledge of his inconstancy, but from knowing he could be so cold and aloof. Far from being her good friend, Jason might have been a callous stranger.

Now she felt a fool for having attempted to appease her faithless lover because a lecher had forced a kiss on her. She had done nothing wrong, yet Jason immediately suspected she had. She gazed defiantly into the glittering depths of his eyes.

A pitiless smile from Jason broke their combatant gazes, then he looked past Helen to where Colin stood.

'I'm not concerned with how you managed to persuade Mrs Marlowe to accompany you, Bridgeman. But I am anxious that you understand you're now *de trop*,' Jason said with eerie placidity. 'Why don't you run along…while you're still able…?'

The smirk writhing on Colin's lips began to wither. Jason Hunter was not a fellow to make idle threats of violence. He had an impressive record with both pistols and sword and was not averse to an impromptu bout of sparring. Colin clearly recalled that Peter Wenham had once riled this fellow enough, by a bit of shabby chicanery, to end sporting a shiner that took the gloss off their friendship for some while.

Bridgeman tilted his head to an arrogant angle, but was already subtly retreating. With a mocking bow for Helen, he turned and began bowling back along the path.

'Do you want me to defend your honour over it? I'll call him out if you like.'

'No…' Helen's eyes were still challengingly fixed on his rugged features etched hard and dark as granite against a backdrop of dusk.

'Did I arrive at an inopportune moment, just as you were sealing the deal with a kiss? Or perhaps you received rather than offered a seduction this time. Is that it?'

Helen flinched beneath his mordant tone, yet answered crisply, 'Yes.'

'Yes…on both accounts?'

'I don't know how you have the nerve to interrogate me over it,' Helen whispered hoarsely. 'Since we became lovers, *I* have thus far slept only with *you.*'

Jason strolled closer to her, halting beneath a little lamp that misted a pale halo above his devilishly dark features. 'I'm pleased to hear it,' he drawled. 'I would be irritated to find I'd been paying for another man's pleasure.'

Helen was stunned by his careless attitude and her glistening eyes lingered on his face.

He gave her an impenitent smile. 'My apologies for being blunt…but, as I recall, we speak plainly, don't we?' he remarked with just a hint of sneering. 'I know his terms won't be more generous than mine. So, tell me, were you preparing to end things between us to claim Westlea House as your own?'

Helen shrivelled inside beneath his ruthless gaze, but managed a controlled response. 'As you have cast me in the role of shameless hussy, I imagine you have already made a decision on it.' She lifted tear-dewed eyes to his face, then blinked furiously. 'I am not about to weep and strive to defend myself,' she whispered with shaky pride. 'I didn't want to take a walk with him. I certainly didn't want him to kiss me, but you may believe what you will about what you saw.' She pulled her shawl tighter about her shoulders and made to sweep past before the mist in her vision became water on her cheeks.

A hand shot out as she came level with him, jerking her close. 'And what I saw was you willingly taking Bridgeman's arm and disappearing with him. You might be naïve, my dear, but even you know men don't invite women to walk these dark pathways so they might talk to them.'

'Talking was exactly *my* intention,' Helen retorted in a shaky tone whilst trying to wrestle her wrist from his grip. 'And if I am naïve, then you must take some of the blame! Having kept company for some weeks with a notorious rake, I imagine that by now I ought be quite jaded!' With a final wrench she freed her wrist and made to bolt past.

'Don't run off, sweet,' Jason said with specious charm as he blocked her path. 'Bridgeman might have abandoned you, but the night's not over yet. If it's corruption you want, I'll give it to you.'

Helen shook her head at him in mute appeal as unbridled lust made dark coals of his eyes. He merely crooked his five fingers at the back of her head, bringing her close. The pretty

string of pearls entwined there scattered to bounce like hail-
stones on parched earth. Momentarily she fought him, then
his mouth took possession of hers with the sensual savagery
she remembered from that first night in his coach. This time
Helen intended tolerating none of it. But traitorous desire,
swift and potent as liquid fire, had started to streak through
her veins. She sensed the tightness in her abdomen and the
drugging pliancy that stole bone from her limbs. Her body was
ready to succumb to the expectation of the pleasure he gave
her. Her jaw was softening, widening to receive his tongue.
Familiar fingers began loosening her bodice and his hands
moulded over the soft mounds of her breasts. In instinctive
response her back arched in unmistakable invitation.

His palms were circling over the hard nubs of her nipples
and despite her weak protestations, her breath was coming in
little gasps. She pleaded for his decency with one tortured
word. 'Jason…'

He laughed against her mouth. 'That's right…it's Jason,'
he breathed harshly. 'Not Marlowe, not Bridgeman. At least
you remembered my name.'

A taunting humour in his voice gave Helen strength to push
him away. When he reached for her again with insolent confidence, a small hand traced an arc to crack hard against a lean
cheek.

He certainly had not been expecting that and Helen took
immediate advantage of his surprise to dart past. She flew
back along the path in the direction of the sound of serenad-
ing violins.

As the dark and quiet were diluted by light and laughter she slowed her pace. Her vibrating fingers forced the buttons on her bodice back into their hooks as she continued to walk out into the milling crowd.

Of the people who had noticed Helen's disappearance, only one now saw her return.

With a twinge of sadness Emily Beaumont watched Helen emerge from the path, quite alone. Her friend's distress was not immediately obvious, but Emily sensed it nonetheless, even before she saw Helen swiftly cuff at her face, then slip into the midst of the throng to lose herself within it. With a murmured excuse for her brother, Tarquin, Emily picked a path towards her.

Emily linked arms with her friend and spontaneously angled her head comfortingly close to Helen's as her fears were confirmed. Helen's lashes were still wet with tears.

Helen gave Emily a faint smile and asked huskily, 'Have you any idea where my brother might be, Emily?'

Emily nodded. 'I have. I'll lead you to him.' She gave Helen's hand a sympathetic pat. 'And you need not fret over Bridgeman's whereabouts. I saw him leave the Gardens looking quite subdued.'

Helen shot Emily a searching look. 'Who told…how did you…?' she stiltedly began.

'Charlotte told me about…the problems,' Emily admitted quietly and gently urged Helen to keep walking. 'You must not blame your sister. She was quite distressed on seeing you go into the walkway with Bridgeman, and blurted it all out to me.' She paused. 'Charlotte was keen to get George to rescue you. She was sure Bridgeman was abducting you. I persuaded her you would be safe, for I had noticed Sir Jason had immediately set off to act knight errant.' Emily slanted a glance at Helen's averted face. 'Sir Jason *did* send Bridgeman packing, didn't he?'

Helen simply nodded and frowned into the distance.

'But…perhaps didn't act very knightly?' Emily suggested, angling her head to see Helen's expression.

'How could he think I was enjoying that horrible man's attention?' Helen bit at her trembling lower lip. 'Is Charlotte somewhere hereabouts with Philip?'

'She and Philip have taken a walk towards the grottoes.'

Helen gave an unconscious little sigh of relief.

'You may tell me to mind my own business if you want to,' Emily said gently. 'But…I know what it is to be the butt of gossip. I also know what it is to be burdened with a brother's selfishness. People might think that I happily tolerate Tarquin's faults. It's not the truth. But he is my brother and I do love him despite all the heartache he causes us.'

Helen turned to give her a wavering smile. 'Where would we be without our families?' she ruefully murmured.

'I think I would be…contentedly raising a brood of children.' Emily divulged that in an ironic tone but Helen sensed it veiled a poignant truth.

Emily answered her unspoken question with a single nod. 'Yes…I would have married a gentleman but for Tarquin spoiling things… Oh, it doesn't matter!' she said briskly. 'It was some years ago now.'

They walked in silence for a moment, then Emily nodded her blonde head. 'There is George and his devoted wife,' she commented acidly. She tugged gently on Helen's arm to slow their pace. 'Before you go, Helen—and I know you will make George take you home—I want you to understand that there is very little that you could tell me that would shock or offend me.'

Helen gave her a long and searching look before saying quietly, 'You are kind, Emily, but, if you knew more about me, I think you would be shocked.'

'And if you knew more about me, I think you would be shocked,' Emily returned. She unlinked their arms and gave Helen a smile. 'So, if you want to talk to someone about any burdensome topic such as…sisters, brothers, lovers…' She caught Helen's eyes in a meaningful gaze. 'You know who to choose.' Quickly she gave Helen's arm a squeeze. 'George has seen us and is coming over.' Helen's brother received a little wave before Emily turned and set off back the way she had come.

Chapter Sixteen

'If you're looking for Mrs Marlowe, you're wasting your time. She's gone.'

Jason pivoted about to see his brother standing behind him with his hands plunged deep into his pockets. 'What do you mean…*gone*?' he demanded in frustration. His eyes narrowed dangerously. 'Did she leave with Bridgeman?'

'Helen went with her brother,' Mark informed soothingly as he strolled closer. 'She looked a little…strained, so I assume he has taken her home.' Mark kept a tactful rein on his curiosity despite being keen to know what had caused Jason's mistress to depart so abruptly. From the dark scowl and unguarded comment thrown at him, he guessed it was due to his heartthrob brother imagining he had a rival.

Mark suppressed a wry smile twitching at his lips. The idea of Sir Jason Hunter—rich as Croesus and devilishly handsome to boot—being jealous of the likes of Colin Bridgeman, who allowedly could boast he had plenty of money if little else, was ludicrous and unprecedented. But when a man was enamoured he acted very oddly. Mark had marvelled before when strong, confident gentlemen of his acquaintance had become enfeebled wretches whilst courting the women they loved.

He had no wish to see his distinguished brother reduced to that pitiful condition, so was ready to act as arbitrator if he could. Despite their fights and arguments, Jason and he were fond of one another.

Mark had never experienced such emotional delirium over a woman, and thanked his lucky stars for it! But then he knew there wasn't a woman alive capable of bringing *him* down.

Oddly, had his attention for the best part of the evening *not* been concentrated on the infuriatingly alluring chit who happened to be Tarquin Beaumont's sister, he might have noticed his brother pursue Helen and Bridgeman into the walkway.

It was through being captivated by Emily Beaumont that he had first sensed something was amiss between his brother and Helen. He had observed Emily flit gracefully through the crowds to gain Helen's side as she emerged, alone, from the dark pathway. Within a moment of them coming together Emily had been discreetly comforting Helen, in the unmistakably tactile way women had. Shortly afterwards Mark had his suspicions confirmed that Helen was upset when a sheepish-looking George Kingston had accompanied his widowed sister to his carriage. Mark had seen Charlotte leaving a few minutes later with Philip and Anne Goode. That party had looked to be in good spirits, indicating they had been in ignorance of Helen's distress.

Mark surfaced from his reflection and noticed Jason was still glaring at the road as though he might conjure up the carriage that had spirited Helen away.

That his brother was in love was indisputable, yet Mark sensed Jason was under the impression he was adequately concealing the strength of his feelings. Even a subtle interrogation was unlikely to extract anything from Jason whilst he was in this mood other than a few choice epithets.

'I take it you'll be leaving now.' Mark was speaking to Jason, but had difficulty removing his gaze from Emily's pensive profile. He heard a grunted affirmative, but it was a moment later that he realised his brother was already striding away towards the exit.

Mark sent a shrewd look at his old friend Tarquin. He hadn't spoken to him yet this evening; it was high time he remedied that.

Tarquin greeted Mark with a thump on the shoulder and immediately drew him into the circle of young bucks. Some of them seemed to be attempting to impress his sister with tales of their prowess in tooling the ribbons. Despite an absent smile here and an abstracted murmur there, Emily still seemed to be locked within her own consciousness…until her brother mentioned the name Hunter.

Emily snapped from her reverie and ran her eyes coldly over the man who had joined them. Within a second her disgust was directed elsewhere, for a couple of young ladies close by had suddenly remembered to say hello to her.

Moira and Felicity Watson had virtually ignored her since

they arrived despite their family group being just a few yards away. Tarquin's incarceration had rendered her *persona non grata* to hypocrites she previously had classed as friends. Now, because Mark Hunter had graced her circle with his presence, the cousins remembered the Beaumonts existed and fluttered close with breathy enquiries of how they all did.

After a terse response Emily showed them an elevated shoulder. It was a manoeuvre that brought her about to again face Mark. She tipped up her proud, heart-shaped face to challenge his stare. Her head bobbed a curt acknowledgement, but her blue eyes were icy with dislike.

Mark absorbed her antipathy and forged a stoic smile. He was sure he didn't give a damn if she liked him or not. He had come over to discover what the hell was going on between Jason and Helen. His brother had left Grosvenor Square earlier that evening in a good mood. The fact that Jason had been more than usually generous with his money and his property since he'd fallen in love was no inconsiderable incentive for Mark to try and smooth things over between the lovers. He had been about to ask to borrow Jason's racing curricle to take him swiftly to Newhaven. A boxing bout with a new French fighter had been arranged and he had promised his cronies, who had arranged to bring over the foreign pugilist on a yacht, that he would put in an appearance on the coast and run the book.

He saw Emily was about to put distance between them, so said in a solemn murmur, 'Forgive me for mentioning a rather delicate matter, but I noticed that you were talking privately to Mrs Marlowe. I have just been similarly occupied with my brother.' A meaningful throb quietened his voice to little more than a murmur. He sighed and shook his head sadly. 'It's a pity when misunderstandings lead to rifts between people who care about one another.' His frank gaze lingered on her face. He could tell she was torn between her loyalty to Helen and a desire to do what she could to restore her friend's happiness.

'Indeed, it is a shame, sir,' Emily breathed tartly. 'But not surprising that such misunderstandings originate in male egotism.'

Mark relaxed a little. If he was careful, he might yet learn what the problem was. 'My brother is proud, I'll admit; but then no man likes being taken for a fool…'

'And no woman likes being taken for a cheat, especially when she had done nothing but try to selflessly protect a sister,' Emily hissed angrily. Suddenly aware that she had said too much she blinked rapidly at her dainty shoes. 'I beg you will please forget that I told you that. I know you are aware, from your brother, what went on. But I would hate either Helen or Charlotte to think I had betrayed them with talking loosely to—'

'To…?' Mark prompted. 'Who am I exactly, Miss Beaumont?' he asked softly. 'Lucifer? Sir Jason's brother? A scoundrel to avoid?'

Emily swallowed. 'You are the man who had my brother thrown in gaol,' she retorted. 'And I do not like you, nor ever will!'

Mark tactically shifted position so that he and Emily were slightly cut off from the rest of the group. 'That is for another time,' he said gently. 'Helen Marlowe is your friend and Jason is my brother. We are simply trying to help reconcile two people. I guess from what you have said that Kingston is hoping to use one of his sisters to keep Bridgeman at bay. Is that it?'

Emily swiftly looked up. *'Is that it?* You did not know?' Her small mouth slackened in shock. 'Oh, you beast! You have tricked me into telling you what you did not know.' She backed away from him a pace, her features contorted in anger, her complexion white as chalk. 'I don't know why I'm surprised,' she choked in a whisper, for her brother had turned about to look at her. 'I always knew you for a blackguard. It was stupid of me to forget, even for a moment.' With that she whipped past him and began to give the nearest of Tarquin's friends her undivided attention.

It was whilst Jason was pacing to and fro on the pavement by his carriage, undecided whether to follow Helen to Westlea House and grovel an apology, or find Bridgeman and let him explain himself…before he knocked his teeth down his throat… that Diana Tucker emerged from the shadows. It was the distinctive perfume she used that first alerted him to her presence. Turning his head, he saw sinuous curls, pale as moonbeams, as she lifted the hood of her cloak.

Diana moved towards him, her hips undulating beneath the light silk of her clothing. She, more than any other, was convinced that Jason and Helen Marlowe were sleeping together.

After all, it could be no coincidence that she had received a parting settlement from her wealthy lover just a few days before he was seen squiring Mrs Marlowe to the opera. The pique she had felt at being so efficiently discarded in favour of a woman older and, in her opinion, far less comely, was still uncontrollable.

But tonight she had realised, with great elation, that all was not well between the lovers. Her eyes had followed Jason most of the evening so she had seen him enter the dark walkway. Constantly watching for his return, she had thus observed Helen hasten out looking tearful. When Jason had stridden out a few minutes later, Diana had been relieved to see his face so grimly set. It had been the fateful incident she needed to approach him and renew their relationship. So, for some minutes, she had been stalking Jason here and there about the Gardens with the sole intention of getting him alone so she might seduce him into taking her back.

He had handsomely pensioned her off with a house and a generous sum of money, but she missed the prestige, and the envy of other women, that came with being mistress to one of the *ton*'s most desirable gentlemen.

'Will you take me home, please, Jason?' Diana huskily entreated. 'I've got separated from my friends and they've left without me. You won't make me hail a hackney, will you?' She slanted up at him a coy smile. She was close to him now, her rounded hip pressing into the hard muscle of his thigh.

Jason leaned back against his carriage door. He nodded along the street to a smart coach fronted by two pairs of splendid thoroughbreds. 'Frobisher's vehicle,' he said succinctly. 'He might have found his senses and decided not to marry your friend, but I'm sure he still likes Mrs Bertram well enough to give her a ride home. If you ask nicely, I expect he'll take you, too.' Jason gave her a cynical smile. He hadn't paid much attention to Diana this evening, but he was well aware that she had arrived with Lord Frobisher's party and had her gallants with her.

Diana pouted up at him. 'I'd rather ask *you* nicely to take me home, Jason. You haven't so soon forgot how very *nice* I can be to you…have you?' She suddenly went on to tiptoe and placed a moist kiss on his lips. His lack of enthusiasm was emphasised by a curse beneath his breath. Wounded by the careless rebuff, Diana nevertheless persisted with her seduction. Her tongue tip darted to tease the lobe of an ear before he forcibly held her away.

'Good evening, *Sir Jason.*'

Jason recognised the voice that had called the sly greeting and he immediately choked a stronger oath. With a brief farewell to his former paramour, he strolled to give instructions to his driver to take him to Grosvenor Square. It was only then he turned to acknowledge Iris Kingston. She was arm in arm with a young fop who looked to be still wet behind the ears. They were given a nod and a curt, 'Good evening,' before he was swiftly in his coach and on his way home.

Iris sent Diana a scoffing smirk, then watched her flounce back towards the Pleasure Gardens. Iris guessed that the common baggage had looked indignant because she had been unsuccessful in luring Jason back to her. But the realisation that he might have spurned Diana because Helen still had her claws in him was irritating. Colin was also in Helen's thrall. In fact, both the affluent gentlemen that Iris wanted at her beck and call were infatuated with her skinny black-haired sister-in-law and it greatly irked.

Iris allowed her youthful escort to nudge her into a gap in the hedge and fumble with her clothes, but even as she murmured encouragement to him, her mind was investigating how she might bring Helen Marlowe down a peg or two.

George Kingston was slumped, semi-conscious, in an armchair, but he raised his bleary eyes as his wife came into the sitting room. A brandy glass was waved at her as he slurred, 'Ah, there you are, m'schweet. Home a' lasht. Join m'in a drink?'

Iris gave him an apathetic glance but did help herself to the decanter. Suddenly she shot a canny look at her husband. He divulged to her very little lately. But he was quite obviously drunk and might just let slip what had occurred to make Helen demand George take her immediately home.

She strolled to the fire and held out her palms to the embers dying in the grate. 'I saw Sir Jason just as we left the Gardens. He was in the Tucker woman's embrace.'

George snuffled a laugh. 'I doan' think so.'

'He was, I tell you,' Iris sweetly remonstrated and playfully tickled George's cheek with a fingertip.

Even intoxicated, George understood his wife well enough

to send her a smile that was deeply cynical. He took a swig of brandy.

'I watched that harlot kissing him in the street. Bold as you please!'

George swished the amber liquid in his glass and shook his head at it. 'Bridgeman's the problem, not her, but Jay hates me still for Beatrice…so p'raps he used Helen…'

Iris's eyes narrowed in interest as she tried to decipher her husband's drunken ramblings. 'Beatrice?' she repeated softly. 'She is Jason's sister, surely.'

George nodded, a shock of dark hair falling lankly towards his nose. 'Schweet Beatrice,' he mumbled into his drink. 'He's never ever forgiven me for that.'

'You seduced her? You seduced Beatrice Hunter?' Iris whispered in astonishment.

George looked up glassily. 'No! An' I din't abduct her either. She came willingly.' He swayed his head and nuzzled the rim of his tumbler. 'Should have let us be. Would have married her…said I would. Made us turn back. Not even half-way to Gretna… Shame…'

Iris stood for some minutes, digesting the information. When next she looked at her husband, she saw George's chin was propped on his chest. She removed the glass from his limp fingers and deposited it on a table. With a slyly satisfied smile on her lips, she took herself off to bed.

Mark Hunter found his older brother in much the same inebriated state as Iris Kingston had found her husband.

Jason, however, being renowned for the ability to imbibe an astonishing amount before keeling over, was more lucid than George had been. Mark eyed the depleted decanter, precariously perched on the edge of the desk in Jason's study. He then took another, deeply respectful, look at Jason. He had seen old Cedric fill to the top the large crystal bottle not an hour before they left the house earlier in the evening.

Jason thrust himself back in his chair and eyed his brother from beneath a lowering brow. He then propped his head against the chair back. 'What time is it?' he asked on a sigh.

'Time you went to bed,' Mark returned easily.

In response to that dictate Jason emptied what was left in the decanter into his glass. He despatched the brandy in a single swallow.

'Not tired, eh?' Mark said drolly. 'In that case…there's something about this evening's fiasco you might like to hear. It concerns that weasel Bridgeman and how he managed to get Helen to go with him.'

Jason snapped his head forward and silently studied his brother with eyes that resembled molten lead. 'I'm listening…'

Jason's deceptively gentle tone of voice sent a *frisson* through Mark's body. At that moment he almost pitied Bridgeman… George Kingston, too. For without a doubt Helen's brother was up to his neck in it all, and a day of reckoning was fast approaching.

* * *

'Mrs Kingston is here to see you, ma'am.'

Helen looked up from the journal she had been idly flicking through. Her heart sank and just for a moment she considered sending Iris away. Obviously the rumour mill had already set to grinding over her hasty departure from Vauxhall Gardens and her sister-in-law had come to pry, or gloat, depending on how much she had managed to discover about what went on.

Charlotte's thoughts of pleading a migraine, or some similar ailment, to avoid seeing Iris were obviously in tune with Helen's.

'Oh, send her away, for Heaven's sake!' Charlotte dropped to the sofa the little handkerchief she had been embroidering and wrinkled her brow at Helen. 'She is only here to quiz us over Bridgeman. Perhaps she saw you disappear with him at Vauxhall. Do you think George has told her he wants to marry me? She's probably jealous. I know she has a fancy for the wretch.'

'I'm sure George has said nothing,' Helen soothed quietly. 'He would not boast of his involvement in such sordid dealings…' In her mind she concluded…but Bridgeman might….

But it was too late for either sister to plead an indisposition, for Iris had grown impatient waiting to be admitted. She barged past Betty and sailed into the room.

Charlotte gave Iris a mumbled greeting, then fidgeted on the sofa for a moment. 'Oh…I recall I've a letter to finish. It's upstairs.' With that Charlotte sprang out of the chair and was soon making her escape.

'Fetch some tea, please, Betty,' Helen commanded from weary hospitality.

Iris stripped off her gloves and removed her stylish bonnet from her neat coiffure. 'You look washed out,' she remarked with a hint of satisfaction. 'And I'm not surprised at all!'

Helen gave her sister-in-law a penetrating look. Iris obviously was hoping a show of faux sympathy might lead to a heart to heart between them. Helen had no intention of telling her a solitary thing, but she took note of the comment on her appearance and tidied the wisps of raven hair that had escaped their pins. She knew she looked pale and tired; it was a consequence of having wept instead of slept for most of the night. 'Is George not with you?' Helen asked simply for something to say. She resumed flicking over pages in the journal.

'No, I didn't want George to come with me. In truth, I'm glad Charlotte is from the room. I wanted to speak to you alone.' Helen received a meaningful stare from blue eyes that watched her from beneath sooty lashes. 'I have something important to tell you and there is no use in being mealy mouthed. First, I shall frankly say that I'm aware you and Jason Hunter are lovers. Or perhaps I should say I'm aware you *were* lovers…' Iris cocked a knowing eyebrow at Helen.

'You said you had something *important* to say…?' Helen coolly returned, despite feeling her cheeks warming.

Iris smiled. 'It's no use coming over prim now. Everybody has guessed you have been carrying on a liaison with him.'

Iris settled back into the sofa and smoothed her skirt. 'I know we have not always seen eye to eye, but I have come to do you a service.' She gazed pityingly at Helen. 'He has treated you cruelly and you ought know why. I'm sure I would not like it at all if a gentleman slept with me simply to avenge a wrong done his sister.'

With a deal of embellishment, if no actual lies, Iris recounted what George had said about his having compromised Beatrice Hunter. She added that George suspected Jason had long harboured a desire to wreak revenge for it.

Whilst that bombshell was causing a stricken look to tauten her sister-in-law's chalky complexion, Iris delivered her pièce de résistance. She solemnly recounted having quit Vauxhall yesterday evening only to see Diana Tucker brazenly kissing Sir Jason by his carriage, in full view of those passing by.

'*We* know she is not a lady…but it was hardly the behaviour expected of a gentleman, either.' Iris took advantage of Helen's silence to add, 'Why…you could not have been gone from him even an hour….'

Chapter Seventeen

'What in damnation are you doing here at this ungodly hour?'

George had his head propped in both hands, his elbows resting on the table, but he had glanced up to deliver that testy remark. He had a hangover that made it seem a blacksmith had set up business inside his skull. A regular thump was affecting his vision and the oak panelling in the dining room seemed nauseatingly atilt. Having sheltered his throbbing brow a few moments longer in his cupped palms he managed to rouse himself sufficiently to bark at his hovering butler to be gone.

'Women or money? It must be one of the two to bring you here so confoundedly early.'

'It's both,' Jason told him and, taking a chair opposite, sat down, uninvited, at the breakfast table.

George wrapped himself tighter into his dressing gown and took a nibble at dry toast. The tasteless morsel did nothing to settle his queasy stomach. His unwelcome visitor was eerily quiet and that started him fidgeting. Silverware was pushed about on mahogany. 'You've found out that I owe that bastard, Bridgeman, money and he's threatening me with the duns. What of it?'

'I found out that you're not averse to pimping to clear your debts.'

George felt fiery heat prickle beneath his silk collar. 'Bridgeman wanted to marry Charlotte,' he snapped, tossing a spoon in irritation. 'If encouraging an eligible fellow makes me a pimp, then every fond mama with a chit to offload is a procuress.'

'And Helen? Did he want to marry her, too?'

George rubbed a hand over his bristly jaw and slanted a proper look at the man opposite. Jason had a similar drink-dissipated appearance to the one he'd seen reflected in his dressing mirror not an hour since. 'You're still too far in your cups...as I am,' he mumbled. 'Best leave this till another time....'

'Did he want to marry Helen, too?' Jason roared.

George started and a hand sprang to his pounding head. 'Of course not! He's wanted her for years, but not as a wife.' George felt the burning on his neck again but managed to sneer, 'He just wanted to sleep with her...same as you....'

Jason violently gained his feet. 'Helen went with Bridgeman last night to try and persuade him to leave Charlotte alone.'

'I know...she told me when I took her home.'

'What else did she say?'

'If you think I'll repeat to you a private conversation and

betray my sister's trust…' A burst of contemptuous laughter interrupted George.

'You've been betraying your sister's trust for years. Helen trusted you to do what your father asked, and care for her and Charlotte. She trusted you to let your sister marry the man she loved.'

'Just as your sister trusted you to let her marry the man she loved,' George spat and pushed himself upright. He stood unsteadily with his fists balled on the table as support. 'But you couldn't do it, could you? You had to spoil it for us.'

Jason walked towards George, his face grimly set. 'Is that what your spite and resentment is all about? You and Beatrice?' he demanded to know.

George's eyes dropped away from the steel-grey stare. In resignation he flapped a hand before showing Jason his back.

A vicious grip on George's shoulder spun him around so they were again face to face. 'My sister was sixteen when you persuaded her to run off. The consequences for her future would have been unspeakable had the scandal leaked out.'

'I would have married her,' George gritted in a voice that had lost none of its belligerent edge.

'She was too young and too innocent and you knew it. But you were always too damned selfish…just as you are now.'

'And you were always too damned horny…just as you are now. Iris told me she saw you kissing Diana last night. You went out for the evening with Helen, but soon found another woman to take her place. Yet you have the gall to come here and act noble on Helen's account!' George jeered.

'Oh, I didn't come here to act noble, George,' Jason softly enunciated. 'I came here to do this.' A single punch knocked George down into his chair. It teetered on its back legs for a moment before crashing over on to the polished parquet and sending George sprawling. 'That's long overdue and not nearly enough. But it'll do for now,' Jason said before quitting the room.

Cedric's rheumy eyes flowed over the neatly dressed young woman. She looked more modish than when last she'd arrived, alone, demanding to see the master. But her haughty look was unchanged.

'Sir Jason's not here,' he told her and started to shut the door.

Helen stepped on to the threshold to prevent him dismissing her. 'Is Sir Jason soon expected back?' she asked firmly.

'Eh?' Cedric cocked his good ear at her.

'Is your master soon expected home?' Helen asked with more volume.

'He might be…' Cedric said unhelpfully. His infirm memory suddenly pounced on something important. He recalled getting a flea in his ear for having treated this chit impolitely last time she came asking for the master. Cedric belatedly dipped his wispy head and opened the door a little wider.

'I'll wait, thank you.' Helen slipped neatly past the old retainer and into the magnificent hallway of Jason's Grosvenor Square residence.

Her heart was beating energetically, deafening her with the

roar of fast-flowing blood and rendering her oblivious to Cedric's mutterings. Fearing he might again put her in the cupboard to wait, she swiftly stepped to a hallway chair and sat down. From under her bonnet brim she watched Cedric give her a stern stare, then move away on slow feet.

Helen watched his shuffling retreat, then closed her eyes as the enormity of what she'd done overwhelmed her. She had again acted with a brazen contempt for etiquette by coming here alone and uninvited. But having found the temerity to act quickly to end their affair, she did not want her courage to ebb away.

Suddenly it occurred to her that Jason might be so early abroad because he had gone to Westlea House to perform the same task as had brought her to see him.

It was finished between them, she understood that, and wanted it that way, but her pride demanded that she be the one to formally conclude their relationship.

Iris and Bridgeman were both spiteful people, but Helen instinctively knew that they had told her facts, not falsehoods. Undoubtedly some of what Iris had said had been intentionally exaggerated and hurtful, but oddly it had been enlightening, too. Pieces of a puzzle had slipped into place concerning the hatred that had sprung up between George and Jason a decade ago. George had compromised Beatrice and made Jason bitter and vengeful. As for Bridgeman exulting that Jason was not faithful to her, she had at the outset of their affair not expected he would be. Bridgeman had simply brought again into focus a wounding truth she had tried to ig-

nore. Despite her boasts in Hyde Park, when she'd propositioned Jason, she had failed miserably to act with sophistication and accept she was to him simply a bed-partner.

Jason had been generous to her, but then he was a wealthy
man who could afford to pay well for his pleasure. He had
been a clever lover but, of course, he had much experience
with a variety of women to draw on. He was courteous and
charming, but then he was with most people—it was in his
breeding. With women he desired, he was essentially the
hard-hearted rake of his notoriety. And she was a perfect fool
to have thought herself capable of tolerating loveless cou-
plings with a man who simply wanted to slake his lust with
a willing woman.

Most of all, she was a fool for knowing it all and still loving him.

Helen felt tears prick at the backs of her eyes and dashed
them away with gloved fingers. She glanced about at her surroundings, apathetically taking in the opulence. Every surface
was polished, every crystal droplet gleaming and every second silent. The last time she'd been here she'd had no opportunity to ponder on elegant furnishings and wonderful
architecture. But his mansion didn't impress her. She would
rather have the shabby comfort of her Westlea House than this
beautiful shell that so well matched its owner.

She collected her thoughts and forced her mind to practicalities. She ought to concentrate on securing her home and
the cash she had been promised…

'Helen?'

Helen jumped to her feet at the sound of her name. So entrenched in her thoughts had she been that she had missed the noise of a key turning smoothly in the lock.

They faced each other for a moment in tense quiet, then Jason closed the door and walked towards her.

Helen desperately blinked away the mist in her eyes and moistened her lips. 'I'm sorry to have come here, but it is too late to fret over gossip, and best that things are swiftly concluded.' She tilted her chin and squarely met his eyes. Her golden glance flitted over his haggard features and crumpled clothes. He looked the worse for a night of roistering, yet was still heartbreakingly handsome. His dishevelment was out of character and made him look boyish and vulnerable. She felt tempted to touch back the knot of locks on his brow.

It suddenly occurred to her that he might not have set out early this morning, but had rather come home late. Perhaps that kiss with Mrs Tucker had led to him spending the night with her. He certainly had the look of a man spent....

Helen winced. And she had been foolish enough to think he might have bothered going out early to see her! Fingers that moments ago had been yearning to soothe him were clenched into fists at her side. She would not be sidetracked by petty jealousy into forgetting to claim what he had agreed to give her.

'Come into the study where we can talk,' Jason urged gently. He absently swiped a hand over the dusky growth on his chin, as though regretting his unkempt appearance.

Helen gracefully glided away, evading his outstretched

hand, then faced him again. The silence, the cool marble surroundings, lent her an air of composure. 'There is no need for me to tarry,' she quietly told him. 'This is private enough and what I have to say will not take more than a moment.' She noted the change in his demeanour as he felt the force of her frigidity.

'I would be grateful if you would arrange for my settlement to be dealt with as soon as possible. And I trust that what happened between us yesterday evening will in no way affect Philip's future prospects. That is all I have to say. Good day to you, sir.' Helen's husky speech had barely concluded before she was stepping past him. She was fumbling to open the huge door when Jason joined her there and smoothly performed the office.

Wordlessly he indicated she should go out. She did so, hastening down the steps. As she reached the bottom and turned towards home, a hand gripped her arm, halting her.

'Get in,' Jason ordered in an uncompromising tone whilst yanking wide his carriage door.

Helen tried to liberate her elbow but his fingers tightened.

'Get in, Helen…please,' he added hoarsely. 'Don't make me abduct you.'

With a sob of frustration Helen gave him a glare but allowed him to help her climb up. With an agile spring that belied his look of enervation, Jason was soon in and sitting opposite her. Storm-grey eyes lingered on her face before he instructed the driver to take them to Hyde Park.

'Why are we going there?' Helen demanded.

'Why not? You seduced me there, it's fitting you discard me there, too.'

His darkly ironic tone brought a tinge of pink to Helen's ivory cheeks. 'I do not find anything amusing in this. You may take me home and nowhere else.'

'Philip and Anne are visiting Charlotte. Are you sure you want to talk there?'

Helen's eyes whipped to him as he settled back into the squabs. 'You have been to Westlea House?'

'Yes.'

'Did you go there to advise me my settlement is being arranged?' Helen whispered.

'No.'

'Why, then?'

'I promised you'd be the first to know if ever I fell in love or wanted to marry.'

She had not for a moment anticipated that. A hand spontaneously sprang to her abdomen to subdue a nauseating lurch. After a long moment she managed to whisper, 'And which is it? Love or marriage?'

'Both.'

'I see. You need not feel obliged to elaborate.' Helen kept her face turned to the street scene. Children playing with a hoop seemed to her quite fascinating. She craned her neck to keep watching them, even though the happy tableau had splintered into fragments. 'I can walk from here, please put me down…'

'Don't you want to know who she is?'

Helen shook her head, fiddled with her bonnet so the brim shielded her face. 'I can guess.' A little laugh bubbled in her aching throat. 'Gossip has started, I'm afraid. This morning my sister-in-law told me she saw you kissing Diana Tucker at Vauxhall.'

'It's not her.' His voice hinted at contemptuous disbelief. 'And I didn't kiss her. It's true she kissed me, and asked me to take her home. I refused and went off on my own.'

Helen swallowed and stole a glance at him. Just as quickly she dragged her eyes away. What did any of it matter now? Nevertheless she could not prevent an acid observation. 'You have the look of a man who has not yet this morning seen his own bed…or his razor or his valet.'

Jason smiled ruefully. 'That's all perfectly true, Helen. But I have seen your brother and Bridgeman this morning. And I have seen Charlotte.'

'You have been to see George? Why?'

'To impress on him how much he disgusts me.' Jason absently flexed the fingers on his right hand.

Helen noticed his scraped knuckles. 'You've hit George? Why? Because of the way he treated Beatrice?'

'No; because of the way he's treated you. And before you ask, yes, Bridgeman felt my displeasure, too.'

'You should not have,' Helen murmured, aghast, simultaneously becoming aware that the coach had drawn to a halt in the park. Sunbeams filtered through branches to warm her face. 'Bridgeman might be vile, but he did not force me to go with him.'

'But he forced his attentions on you.'

'You would not believe my word yesterday evening when I told you that, but you believe him!' Helen angrily blinked teary eyes. 'Is your conceit soothed from knowing I didn't willingly endure that kiss?'

'I know I've been a fool, Helen,' Jason quietly admitted. 'But I was jealous.'

'Jealous of Bridgeman?'

'No…not really.' Jason's tousled head dropped forward and a hand spanned his brow. 'It's not him.' The words emerged through muffling fingers that massaged at his face

'Who, then?' Helen demanded in shock.

'Harry Marlowe.'

Helen stared searchingly at him. When he continued to rub his weary features, she reached to pull his hand away. 'Why? Why are you jealous of Harry?' she asked as her golden eyes scanned his beautifully dissolute face.

'Because you love him, and you were his wife, and that's what I want.' Jason suddenly flung himself back against the seat. 'Don't look so petrified, Helen,' he said with quiet self-mockery. 'I know I can't make you love me, or marry me. I'll marry you on your terms, or continue to protect you. But if you want me out of your life for good, I won't bother you again.' He fell silent, staring through the carriage window. A muscle leaped by his mouth, then he turned to her. 'I'll arrange for the transfer of the deeds.' With that gruff proclamation he abruptly opened the door. 'Graves will take you home. I'll walk.'

Helen slid speedily towards him on the seat. Quickly she closed her fingers over his on the handle. Their faces were so close now she could see the glisten of moisture in his eyes. 'You went to Westlea House this morning to tell me that you love me and want to marry me?'

He said nothing, just continued to look at her. But she could read the truth in his soulful long-lashed eyes.

Helen gave him a shy smile and a hand fluttered to cup his stubbly cheek. 'I won't ever love Harry less...but I think, in time, I might love you more.'

Jason's eyes closed and his face sought the shelter of her cradling palm.

It was when the hot salt stung her skin that she launched herself at him, forcing him back onto the seat. She clung fiercely to his neck and covered his face with tiny kisses. Settling herself on his lap, she murmured, 'I love you, Jason. I love you so much. You've been so kind and generous...'

Helen felt herself unceremoniously tipped on the seat behind him and Jason loomed over her. 'I don't want your gratitude. Just tell me again that you love me,' he demanded in a voice that was rough with need.

'I love you... I think I always have...even when I was a girl.'

His mouth plunged on to hers, hard and warm. It was a kiss like no other they had shared...not skilful or calculated. It was, Helen realised, with a sense of serenity, simply raw adoration.

Jason raised his head, his self-conscious smile betraying that he knew he'd been clumsy.

Helen wound her arms about his neck, keeping him reassuringly close.

'I'll get a special licence. Do you mind if it's a quiet affair, and soon?'

Helen shook her head. 'I've nothing planned for tomorrow,' she said teasingly.

'Tomorrow might do,' he said quite seriously. 'Do you want to go for a walk? Or to Westlea House? We must make arrangements,' he continued in a husky, urgent voice.

Helen nestled her head against his shoulder, feeling utterly content and blissful. 'I'd rather you took me to Chelsea, Jason,' she suggested softly.

Chapter Eighteen

'You're very good at this.'

'You bring out the best in me, sweetheart.'

Helen gave him a speaking look and turned her head on the pillow.

Jason supported his weight on brawny forearms, dipping his head to nudge Helen's face up to his and take her lips in a wooing kiss. His eyes, dark with desire, meshed with hers and he smiled crookedly. 'It's true…' he softly emphasised. 'You bring out the best in me…just you…no one else.' His thumb traced gently where his mouth had plundered hers and plumped the skin to dual scarlet bows. 'Do you believe me, Helen?' Jason asked gently. 'This is unique, I swear.'

She swung back her head, coating his fingers with the black silk of her hair. 'Yes, I believe you. But…'

'But…?'

'I've been jealous, too,' she quietly admitted whilst watching one of her fingers caress the lean flesh of his hand. 'It was silly of me to say that I would not care if you did not devote yourself exclusively to me.' She curled the stroking finger back into her palm. 'In fact, I have been tormented, thinking of you doing this with someone else.'

'I have not, Helen.' Jason's voice was thick with reassurance. 'I swear to you that since we first went to Hyde Park together I've not been with another woman.'

Helen swung her face back and her eyes clung to his. 'Mrs Tucker still lives in one of your houses.'

'Who told you that? Was it George making more mischief?'

'No. Bridgeman taunted me with it. He said Diana was still ensconced in one of your houses.'

'Bridgeman knows nothing,' Jason said with a scornful laugh. 'Had he bothered to check his facts, he would have found out that the property is now Diana's. I gave it to her as a parting gift.' Jason's mouth set grimly. 'I wish now I had not let Bridgeman off so lightly when I saw him earlier. Just for upsetting you over that he deserved another—'

Helen placed a finger on his lips. 'Hush, or I will think you a ruffian to get into two scraps in one day.' She suddenly chuckled. 'But I'm glad you hit Bridgeman, he deserved it…horrible man. He would have tried to coerce Charlotte into marriage and thought nothing of it. And he tried to intentionally hoodwink George with his contract. I don't want George to go to gaol.'

'He won't. I've paid Bridgeman his money.'

Helen hugged him in gratitude then ran loving fingers over the ridges on his chest, luxuriating in the touch of silken skin sheathing rough muscle. 'So a notorious rake has been faithful to me, has he?'

'Absolutely.'

Helen undulated unconsciously beneath him in cat-like contentment. Their slick skin was bonded, their sated bodies still in congress, yet she felt the stirring inside her that told her he was ready to love her again. She felt the warm rush of excitement that made her breasts heavy and her hips instinctively tilt. 'I'm a wanton,' she sighed huskily and nipped his shoulder with teasing teeth.

'Obviously I bring out the best in you,' Jason murmured suggestively.

'You do…but Harry will always have a place in my heart. Do you mind?'

Jason shook his head. 'I'm glad you were happy with him. But I'll make you happier…'

'I wish George was happy.' Helen sighed. 'I know he is a selfish schemer, but it is hard to hate one's own kin. And now I know what it is that has made him so sour.' She met Jason's smouldering eyes. 'I never guessed about him and Beatrice, you know. I had heard that you fell out over a woman, but that was all I knew.' She frowned. 'I imagined Beatrice stayed away from Charlotte's betrothal party because she had guessed about us and wanted to avoid me. It was George she didn't want to see, wasn't it?'

'Yes.' Jason twisted a smile. 'In fact, as soon as she heard George was in town with his wife, she found an excuse to return home.'

'Does she hate him?'

'Actually, I think she still has a scrap of tender feeling for him. Perhaps I was wrong and I should have let them be.' Jason grimaced indecision. 'At the time my mother was distraught and imagining all sorts of ruination and disaster. I couldn't be sure George would act honourably and, had the marriage not taken place, Beatrice's reputation would have been irreparably sullied. She was only sixteen.' Jason gave a sigh. 'He should not have done it…and it is pointless dredging it up—nothing can be changed. But I hope, as brothers-in-law, we might again be friends.'

'I would like that,' Helen said, a little wistfully, for something else was troubling her. 'When Iris told me of it this morning she said you were bitter over it all and that's why you took me for your mistress…as an act of revenge.'

'You don't believe that, do you?'

Jason's voice held such arrant scorn that Helen quickly shook her head.

Jason forked long fingers over Helen's sharp little chin, keeping her facing him. 'It's utter rubbish, not least because, if I'm truthful, I never held George wholly responsible for what went on.'

'Beatrice happily went with him?'

'Yes…but that is not exactly what I meant.' He slanted her a crooked smile. 'George didn't start the madness of lusting after teenage sisters, I did. I told him during a drunken spree, sometime in our misspent youths, that I found you attractive. He then declared that he felt the same way about

Beatrice.' He gave Helen a wry smile. 'I wanted you, but I would never have acted on it. George took it further. He and Beatrice started meeting secretly. Then one night they eloped.' A gentle finger traced a curve on Helen's cheek. 'Had I never admitted to that secret yearning for you, perhaps George would have controlled his feelings until Beatrice was older.'

Helen gazed up at him with wide golden eyes. 'You wanted to marry me when I was fifteen?'

Jason subdued a wolfish smile. 'No…when I was twenty-four I never thought about marriage. But I certainly thought about—'

Helen gave his arm a silencing thump to spare her further blushes. 'I had a crush on you, too. *My* intentions were honourable,' she said, mock-prim. 'I dreamed of marrying you.'

'And now you are.'

'And now I am,' Helen echoed softly, wondrously. A wounding memory haunted her mind. 'Bridgeman called me Hunter's whore and said other people were saying it, too. He never imagined you would make me your wife.'

Jason dipped his head to tenderly kiss away her sadness. 'I think I fell in love with you from the moment you opened the door to me at Westlea House. You looked like a little waif.' He threaded his bruised fingers through the silky black tresses crumpled on the white linen. 'It didn't matter that you were shabbily dressed or had your hair loose. I thought I had never seen a woman as beautiful. I delayed making you my mistress because I intended you to be my wife, Helen.' He kissed her with seductive sweetness. 'Why worry what's been said? We know you've always been Hunter's Lady....'

Epilogue

'Miss Beaumont.'

Emily turned her head on hearing her name. Her heart started to thud as she saw the identity of the gentleman approaching. Not that her odd excitement sprung from liking him, rather he unsettled her.

'Mr Hunter,' she greeted him and sketched a polite bob.

Mark Hunter studied the fair face turned up to his. 'I haven't seen you since the wedding. I think we ought take a little credit for bringing about that very happy occasion.'

Emily immediately smiled at the reference to Helen and Jason's nuptials, and the prior events at Vauxhall Gardens. 'The whole day was wonderful, was it not? Even the weather was glorious.'

'They deserved the best.'

Emily nodded vigorously, her blonde hair rippling prettily. 'Oh, indeed,' she agreed. A silence developed between them so she made conversation as they walked on towards the water in Hyde Park. 'I hope Charlotte's wedding next month is just so blessed with everything good.'

Mark smiled. 'They have Westlea House as a wedding gift. That's certainly good.'

'It will be quite a beautiful home when the work is finished. Charlotte and Philip are lucky indeed to have such a generous brother-in-law.'

'I think perhaps the pair owe thanks to Helen for their good fortune. I know she wanted the newlyweds to have a home of their own.'

'It must be hard to start married life with no privacy, surrounded by one's family.' Emily had said that quite pensively and her eyes instinctively slanted to her brother, who was grouped close by with his friends. She frowned and began to turn away.

Mark glanced at Tarquin, too, and understood why Emily had suddenly withdrawn from him. Tarquin Beaumont was in the company of a notorious gamester and money was clearly changing hands.

Emily was about to fly to her brother's side to attempt to keep him from more trouble. Annoyed that he was to lose her enchanting company, Mark said gruffly, 'Your brother must discipline himself and learn what company to avoid. It is not something you can do for him.'

Emily whipped her head about to give him a haughty stare. 'I quite agree he should pick his friends carefully. I recall you were the Judas who had him thrown in the Fleet.'

'If you will let me explain, there are things you don't know about that,' Mark said on a sigh.

'I know enough,' Emily countered icily. 'I certainly know I do not like you, Mr Hunter, and no sweet talk will change my mind.' Within a moment she had spun on a heel and headed off towards her brother.

Mark Hunter watched her go, an odd expression, part amusement, part exasperation, on his face. 'And I know, Miss Beaumont, that if I wanted to change your mind, it wouldn't be through conversation….

HISTORICAL ROMANCE™

Novels coming in April 2006

THE ROGUE'S KISS
Emily Bascom

Under cover of darkness, a highwayman silently waits.
He is soon to discover that the approaching carriage holds a
beautiful woman – travelling alone. Lady Roisin Melville is
escaping London and the fortune-hunting gentlemen of the *ton*
– only to be held up by a masked figure. With her gun trained
on this daring rogue, can Roisin persuade him to take nothing
more than a kiss…?

A TREACHEROUS PROPOSITION
Patricia Frances Rowell

He trusted no one, and that was his strength – until a brutal
murder linked his life with that of the victim's widow. Vincent
Ingleton, Earl of Lonsdale, found himself drawn to Lady Diana
Corby's haunting vulnerability. But could she ever really love a
man whose whole life was a tissue of deception and danger…?

ROWAN'S REVENGE
Jane Francis

Owain ap Rowan had sworn to track Lady Catherine down.
And in Spain he believed he had finally found her. Her guilt
was obvious – no innocent lady would disguise herself as a boy!
But could he be sure that the beautiful Kate was, in truth, the
lady he sought? With so many secrets between them, he must
not yield to her seductive spell…

MILLS & BOON®

Live the emotion

HIST0306 HB

HISTORICAL ROMANCE™

Another exciting novel available this month is:

THE MISSING HEIR
Gail Ranstrom

What was a buckskin-clad savage doing in her
elegant library? Grace Forbush found it hard to
believe this dangerous-looking stranger could
possibly be an English gentleman – *and* her
late husband's intended heir.

Adam Hawthorne had no time for social niceties. He
was on the trail of the traitor who wanted him dead.
But Grace intrigued him. Why did such a proper lady
play in the worst gaming hells of London? What was
she keeping secret? Was she someone he could trust
when danger threatened them both?

REGENCY

MILLS & BOON®

Live the emotion

HIST0206 HB TMH

THE GLADIATOR'S HONOUR

Michelle Styles

A hardened survivor of more than a dozen
gladiatorial combats, Gaius Gracchus Valens's raw
masculinity fuels many women's sexual fantasies.
He is a man outside polite society, and Roman
noblewoman Julia Antonia knows she should have
nothing to do with a man who is little more than
a slave.

But, with a wisp of scandal clinging to her stola, she is
drawn inexorably towards the forbidden danger
Valens represents. Julia is a tantalising reminder of
the life he had torn from him. To claim her, Valens
must fight one final time – and win!